"Don't you see, Jill?"

Spence turned toward her, his expression both eager and serious. "Don't you see how it's all working?"

"I see that I'm on a runaway train with Charlie Hartman as the engineer," she replied. "I have to know where I'm going, Spence. I can't afford any more detours in my life."

Spence drew her toward him. "This is no detour," he murmured, angling his head for a kiss. "This is an eight-lane interstate."

Her sigh served as agreement, and he proceeded with a kiss that transformed agreement to charged passion.

"Come on," he whispered against her lips. "Let's go get comfortable."

"I hadn't noticed we were uncomfortable," she said, breathing raggedly.

"Maybe not," he said, leading her toward the bedroom, "but we sure are vertical."

Dear Reader:

Last year Temptation and Vicki Lewis Thompson brought you *Be Mine, Valentine*, a charming romance with a little something special. That "something" was Charlie Hartman . . . alias St. Valentine. Now, back by popular demand, Charlie is working his magic on yet another unsuspecting couple. We hope you enjoy the fun as, once again, Charlie lets fly with Cupid's arrow in *Forever Mine, Valentine*, the Temptation Editor's Choice for February.

And remember . . . just when you least expect it you might find a Charlie Hartman in your life. Happy Valentine's Day!

The Editors

Forever Mine, Valentine
VICKI LEWIS THOMPSON

Harlequin Books

TORONTO • NEW YORK • LONDON
AMSTERDAM • PARIS • SYDNEY • HAMBURG
STOCKHOLM • ATHENS • TOKYO • MILAN

Published February 1990

ISBN 0-373-25388-5

1

JILL STOOD in front of the camping supply store and plotted ways to sell the manager on painting his window for Valentine's Day. *You've backpacked your way into my heart.* Nope. *Warm her heart with a Coleman stove.* Ugh. *My canteen runneth over with love.* Yuck!

Of all the stores in this mall, Jegger Outfitters promised to be the toughest sell, but she liked challenges. Maybe she'd walk in without a specific window plan, and if the manager sounded the least bit interested, she'd come up with an idea on the spot. Sometimes pressure could be inspirational. That's how she'd snared the optometrist, with her sudden brainstorm of *Give her rose-colored glasses for Valentine's Day.*

Jegger Outfitters smelled of canvas, crepe soles and pine shelving. Old-fashioned picks and shovels hung on the walls, along with tins for gold panning, old mining claim maps and a ragged banner that vowed Pikes Peak or Bust. In the merchandise on the rustic shelves were several camping items she could have used, but she was here to sell, not buy.

As she continued down the aisle toward the rear of the store, she overheard an angry voice and a placating one coming from behind a closed door marked Private. Damn. Store managers with problems seldom wanted their windows painted with hearts and flowers.

Just then a thin young man in a rumpled cotton shirt and parachute pants rounded a counter and came toward her. "Can I help you?" he asked.

"My name's Jill Amory. I'd like to see the manager please. I think," she added as the tirade from behind the door continued, punctuated by an occasional distinct "Dammit, Charlie," or "She's crazy."

"Uh . . ." The clerk hesitated and followed the line of her gaze.

"This seems like a bad time. Perhaps I could—"

"No," he said quickly, assessing her with a glance. "I wouldn't want to make that decision for him."

"Thanks, but I could easily come back tomorrow. I'm taking orders for valentine window decorations, and it's really no trouble for me to come back." Jill was certain rejection lay behind that office door.

"No," the young man said again, continuing to appraise her from behind wire-rimmed glasses. "Stay right there and I'll tell him you're here."

His blatant perusal didn't disturb Jill; she was used to being ogled. In tandem with orders for window decorations had come several offers for coffee and/or drinks from the male managers she'd approached. Her polite refusals hadn't lost her a single order, which delighted her, confirming that in the past seven months she'd learned to deal effectively with predatory men.

The clerk rapped on the closed door and without waiting for clearance, opened it. "Someone to see you, Spence," he said.

"Who is it?" The voice was still gruff with anger.

"Jill Amory. She wants to decorate the windows for Valentine's Day."

Through the open door Jill heard a bark of laughter. "Has she cleared this with Tippy the Lip?"

"I didn't ask."

"Well, I don't think—"

Jill sighed, knowing what would come next.

"Wait a minute, Spencer, my boy," interrupted a second, older-sounding male voice. "Horace, did you say her last name was Amory?"

"I think that's what she told me, Charlie," the clerk said. "You know her?"

"No, but the name is . . . nice. Is she, ah, young?"

"Maybe early twenties."

"That's young," said the older man, chuckling. "Spencer, couldn't you at least find out what she has in mind?"

Jill was grateful for this unknown Charlie who thought she had a nice name and wanted to give her a chance. At that point the clerk lowered his voice and she heard only snatches of his comments. "Foxy-looking brunette," came through pretty clearly, though.

"Okay." The man named Spence sounded weary. "Send her back."

The clerk stepped out of the office and motioned to Jill. Clutching her scrapbook of Polaroids showing samples of her work, she walked toward the open door. The clerk gave her a thumbs-up signal and returned to his position behind the cash register as she entered the office.

Both men stood, and the man behind the sleek oak desk held out his hand. "Ms Amory? I'm Spence Jegger, and this is my sidekick Charlie Hartman. What can I help you with?"

Jill smiled her way automatically through the introduction, but one look at Spence Jegger told her that he could be trouble. He had a shaving-commercial face—square-cut jaw, strong nose, high forehead. His short brown hair waved just enough to give it shape, and his green turtleneck and jeans revealed an athlete's physique. Jill hoped that Spence Jegger was unavailable.

She watched his brown eyes widen in appreciation as he looked at her and she hoped her reaction hadn't been as obvious as his. She'd traveled through thirty-three states so far and managed to avoid romantic entanglements in every one. With her goal only fifteen states away, she couldn't let an attractive man stop her now.

She turned and shook hands with his friend Charlie, a sweet-looking old guy in a red vest and bow tie. "Please sit down," Charlie said, indicating one of two chairs in front of Spence's desk. "We were just discussing what an interesting name you have. 'Amory' means loving, of course, and here you are to paint valentine decorations on windows. Quite fitting, I should say." He beamed at her. "You appear surprised, my dear. Weren't you aware of your name's origin?"

"Um, no, I wasn't." Jill sank to the upholstered chair and tried to get her bearings. Discussing the origin of her name was a strange beginning for a sales call. "I decorate windows for every holiday, not just Valentine's Day," she said, opening her scrapbook and turning it so that Spence could see. "Here are examples of other windows I've done."

Spence pulled the scrapbook across the desk and leafed through it. "Good work," he said.

"Of course she does good work," Charlie said, not even glancing at the pages. "I could tell that immediately."

Jill stared at him. She hadn't felt such unconditional acceptance from another human being since she'd left Maine and her beloved G.G. "I appreciate your confidence, Mr. Hartman."

"Call me Charlie, my dear. I believe we're going to be great friends."

"Um, that would be nice." Jill decided not to mention that she'd be leaving Colorado Springs in a week or so. If Charlie helped clinch this sale, she'd be his great friend, briefly.

Charlie touched her arm and lowered his voice to a conspiratorial whisper. "Spencer's last name means 'witness our love.'" He waggled his eyebrows at her.

"I heard that, Charlie," Spence said, still turning the pages of the scrapbook. "Knock it off."

"But, my boy, I merely thought . . ."

"I know what you thought." Spence closed the book and passed it back to Jill. "He's a terrific guy, and a heck of a chess player, but he has this habit of trying to orchestrate my love life."

Jill gulped. She'd met some strange ones in the past seven months, but these two took the prize, hands down. "I see." She managed a weak smile. "Would you—would you care for a window decoration, Mr. Jegger?"

"Spencer, I recommend that you—"

"Charlie, now that's really enough," Spence said, frowning at the old man. "Valentine's Day and camping haven't much to do with each other, Ms Amory," he said, turning back to her. "Seems to me that painting the windows of the store for this holiday would be a waste of time and money. Now Memorial Day is a different story. If you'll leave your card, I'll be glad to contact you at the end of April."

"Unfortunately I won't be here then," Jill said, wondering if Charlie's matchmaking efforts had hurt her chances more than they'd helped.

"Oh. Well, Fourth of July is another good holiday for us, and Labor Day. Winter is the slow season for camping gear," he added almost apologetically. "I'm sure you understand. But I'd be glad to take your card for future reference."

Jill liked him for trying to be nice. "I don't have a card," she said. "The truth is, I'm working my way through each of the contiguous forty-eight states by painting holiday window decorations. Once I leave Colorado Springs in a few days, I won't be back."

Beside her, Charlie groaned. "Impossible," he muttered and covered his face with his hands.

Spence seemed to ignore his friend's distress and leaned across the desk. "No kidding? You're making this trip all by yourself?"

"Yes."

"How long have you been on the road?"

"Seven months," Jill replied. From the corner of her eye she noticed that Charlie had come out from behind his hands and was showing interest in the conversation. "I started in Maine, my home state, and Colorado is number thirty-three. I have fifteen to go."

"But not Alaska and Hawaii, I take it," Spence commented.

Jill shook her head. "My old VW van wouldn't make it over the Alaskan Highway, and I can't afford Hawaii."

"Is it some sort of charity promotion?" Spence asked.

Jill had a feeling that if she said yes, she'd get the valentine window order, but she couldn't lie to make a sale. "No, it's a personal thing. I promised myself I'd do this and finish the trip before my twenty-fifth birthday."

"Which is?"

"June twelfth," Jill replied.

"My goodness," Charlie said, straightening. "You have plenty of time remaining. Why not stay on here a bit longer? Colorado Springs is a beautiful city, and you can't begin to see it all in a few days, can she, Spencer?"

Jill picked up her scrapbook and stood. Enough was enough. "Thank you both for your time," she said, "but I must stay on schedule. Now if you'll excuse me, I have more sales calls to make before I begin painting tomorrow." Ignoring Charlie's frantic signals to Spence, she turned to leave.

"Ms Amory," Spence called when she was halfway to the door.

"Yes?" She pivoted.

Although Charlie sat upright, his gaze intent on her, Spence leaned back in his chair with easy nonchalance. "Just for curiosity's sake, how would you tie Valentine's Day in with what I have to sell?" he asked.

She hesitated. Why not tell him she had no idea and leave? End of story. End of danger. To her dismay, an answer popped out. "How about a bright red sleeping bag for two?"

His eyebrows rose and he looked amused. "I'll admit I hadn't thought of that."

Jill wished fervently that she hadn't, either. The devil had taken her tongue. Charlie watched them silently, following the conversation like a spectator at a tennis match.

"And how would you depict a double sleeping bag on the window?" he asked. "This is a G-rated store. Little kids come in here all the time."

"Forget the sleeping bag. It was a terrible idea," she said, her cheeks turning valentine red. Charlie was smiling. "Socks," she blurted. "Thermal socks would be a loving gesture. Maybe with a slogan like *Warm her from heart to toe on Valentine's Day*."

"Catchy." Spence's brown eyes twinkled. "How much would you charge for this window painting of hearts and toes?"

"Thirty dollars," Jill said quickly, "for both windows. And I'll dream up more than the socks idea. Maybe long underwear, in red . . ."

"Watch it. You're straying into R-rated territory again," Spence said with a smile. "I swear I never considered camping gear sexy, but you're changing my mind."

"Let's forget the whole thing," Jill said. "You were right the first time. Valentine's Day and camping gear don't mix."

"No, no." Spence protested. "I'm getting into this. It's a terrific idea. I can hardly wait. When will you start?"

She'd done it now. "Well, I've sold window decorations to twenty-one stores on the top floor, and doing those will take me a couple of days, at least. I've been telling people on the lower level to plan for about three days' wait."

"Too bad."

"I can see the delay bothers you," she said with relief. "But I can't work any faster, so perhaps we should just cancel the order."

"No way. I'll wait. A schedule's a schedule. Right, Charlie?"

Charlie's grin was so wide that it barely fitted on his face. "Right, my boy."

"So I'll see you in three days." Spence held out his hand. "Thanks for dropping by."

She automatically took his hand. "You're welcome. See you in three days."

"Goodbye, my dear," Charlie said. "And you can expect to see me sooner than three days. I'm likely to materialize anywhere in the mall. I'm certain we'll run into each other, and I'd like to become better acquainted."

"It's a nice thought, Charlie." She shook his hand, too. "But I really will be leaving town in a week."

"Ah, yes, well . . ."

Jill knew from the conspiratorial gleam in his eyes that he didn't believe a word of it. But she would leave. G.G. was counting on her to send postcards from every state capital, and Aaron was counting on her to come home on time. But most of all, Jill would finish the trip for herself. Nobody, not even a kind old gentleman like Charlie Hartman, would stop her.

THE NEXT MORNING Jill parked her van in the vast Remembrance Mall parking lot. The first time she'd seen it, the mall had reminded her more of a theme park than a shopping center. In all her travels and with all her window painting, she'd never worked in anything quite like this two-tiered structure. She'd spent her first day there just exploring the place.

Victorian gingerbread in gay pastels covered everything, both inside and out, echoing the fashion of Colorado's gold rush days. Inside the mall, shoppers strolled down an eighteen-nineties avenue, complete with globe streetlamps and striped awnings over the storefronts.

In a center courtyard on the bottom floor nestled a skating rink designed to look like a backwoods pond surrounded with fallen logs for sitting and miniature gas-fueled campfires for warming cold hands and feet. Jill had expected to see women in long skirts and muffs twirling on the ice, but instead teenagers in jeans and leg-warmers reminded her that this was indeed the twentieth century.

A scaled-down trolley system ran the length of the bottom floor. The conductor, complete with handlebar mustache, gave seats to the elderly and the handicapped before allowing children or able-bodied adults to ride. On the top floor, instead of a trolley, motorized buggies provided transportation for the handicapped.

A large retail space on that floor housed a museum where people wandered free of charge among artifacts from the late nineteenth century. Nearby, a melodrama theater supported by amateur theatrical groups took their revenue from what the audience dropped into a bowler hat after each performance. Jill was thoroughly charmed with the Remembrance Mall and would have enjoyed the days she spent there no matter what her task.

The stores were opening for the day when she notified the manager of the Sweet Delights Confectionery that she was ready to begin. After taking off her coat, she unpacked her acrylics and brushes and started to work.

She outlined a lace heart in blush pink before reaching for a pot of white to begin a delicate border of more lace. The candy-shop manager had been specific about the valentines she wanted painted on her display windows. They were to look old-fashioned, in keeping with the flavor of the Remembrance Mall.

"Nice job." The speaker, a man, sounded out of breath.

Jill glanced up and recognized the retreating form of Charlie Hartman. He walked briskly down the mall away from her, his arms working like pistons as he churned along in the company of several other men and women about his age. With the exception of Charlie, all of them wore sweat suits in Easter-egg colors.

Must be the Senior Striders, Jill thought with a smile. She'd noticed them a couple of days earlier and had asked a shopkeeper who they were. She'd discovered that about twenty seniors race-walked through the mall on Mondays, Wednesdays and Fridays. She hadn't seen Charlie among them then, but he might have been there; she hadn't studied them closely.

Either Charlie hadn't figured out the Senior Striders' dress code or didn't care for it, Jill mused as she gazed after him. With his leather-elbowed tweed sport coat and his jaunty fedora, he looked like a university professor late for class.

She returned to her work, determined to make this window, her first in the mall, a masterpiece. She'd found that reluctant store managers often capitulated after watching her create something wonderful for another business.

"Needs some red," gasped Charlie as the Senior Striders whisked by again some minutes later.

"I'd planned on it," Jill called after him. Then she laughed at herself, because she hadn't planned on it, at least not consciously. Sidewalk superintendents often showed up while she was working, but she'd never had one fling comments as he spun past her like a geriatric wind-up toy.

She looked at her watch and estimated when he'd be back. The middle of the lace heart was dry, so she picked up her red paint and brushed in a small heart in the center of the larger one. The old man was right, she thought, stepping back to gauge the effect; the valentine had needed some red.

From the corner of her eye she saw the colorful blur of Senior Striders rounding the bend. Turning her head, she watched them approach with Charlie bringing up the rear. For the first time she noticed that his clothes were a little on the shabby side, except for a snowy pair of running shoes that looked fresh off the shelf. Jill thought she remembered a pair just like them in the shoe section at Jegger Outfitters.

"How do you like it?" she asked, gesturing toward the window when he was within earshot.

"Capital, my dear," he puffed. "Just capital."

"Charlie, you're lagging," a spry woman called over the shoulder of her purple sweat suit.

"Yes, well, I have business here," Charlie said, breathing hard as he stopped next to Jill. "I'll fall in on the next go-round, Gladys."

"That's no way to trim your gluteus maximus, Charlie," the woman warned in a tone like a door chime. Then she sped away with the others.

"Whew." Charlie took out a handkerchief and mopped his ruddy face. Then, seemingly as an afterthought, he polished a gold figure-eight pin fastened to his lapel before returning the handkerchief to his coat pocket. "I felt certain that these professional shoes would put me in the middle of the pack, so to speak," he said, glancing at his feet, "yet I'm still the hindmost member of the Senior Striders." He winked at Jill. "Perhaps when they come around again I'll set out in front of them. That would be nice, to lead for a change."

"I thought you were exercising, not competing," Jill said.

"Technically, yes. But I can tell that Gladys expects a better showing of me than always being last."

"Is Gladys your wife?"

The old man's red face turned even redder. "Goodness, no. She's merely a, uh, a friend."

"Oh." Jill smiled, suspecting a romance. "That's nice."

"Actually, it's a bit of a sticky wicket, as the British say, but that's neither here nor there. I'm glad to see you again, Miss Jill Amory."

"I'm glad to see you, too, Charlie." And she discovered that she was. She couldn't understand why she had Charlie's wholehearted approval, but it felt good, whatever the reason. "You remind me of someone back home, someone I miss a lot."

"And who might that be?"

"My great-grandmother. I call her G.G."

"How quaint," Charlie said with a smile.

"Of course you're probably not old enough to be my great-grandfather," she added, hoping she hadn't offended him.

"I dare say that I am. Quite old enough." Charlie stepped aside as a motorized cart carrying an elderly couple passed by.

"Yet you're race-walking, and that pair there needs special transportation," Jill said.

"Ah, but everyone's situation is different, my dear. No telling what sort of hardships that couple has endured. No doubt they deserve to ride. I only hope they'll continue to have the chance."

"What do you mean?"

Charlie rubbed his chin and gazed after the cart. "The new mall management wants to do away with the free carts and the trolley. People will have to produce chits to prove they've bought something if they expect a ride."

"Really? What a shame. I admired the way this mall provided for the elderly and the handicapped shoppers."

Charlie gazed at her approvingly. "I rather thought you'd feel that way. So does Spencer. He's battling with Tippy the Lip—I mean, Ms Henderson—to stop these insane cost-cutting measures."

"Tippy the Lip," Jill said with a grin. "I remember hearing that name yesterday and wondering who it was."

"Have you met Ms Henderson?"

"Yes, when I got permission to sell window decorations in the mall."

"Spencer's epithet is well deserved. I've never met a woman with such an abrasive manner of speaking."

Jill laughed. "I know what you mean. She really turned me off, too, and I wondered how such a woman could have dreamed up all the wonderful features of this mall."

"Obviously they were dreamed up by her predecessor, with some help from the Jegger family. Spencer's parents once owned the land this mall was built on. According to Spencer, Jegger's has been an institution since the gold rush days, and his parents hesitated to sell the land and tear down the original store. The only reason they agreed was because the developers had such humanitarian concepts. Now Spencer's in the position of having to fight to keep them."

"Good for him," Jill said, impressed in spite of herself. "How's he doing?"

"Not very well. He's had several nonproductive meetings with Ms Henderson and they always end in shouting matches, apparently."

"He ought to organize the other store owners. I remember a shopping center in North Dakota where the tenants protested against poor maintenance and trash collection. Their demands were met because they stuck together."

Charlie's face lit up and he nodded. "You might mention that to Spencer when you see him. Were you able to observe how the tenants worked together for this end?" he added casually.

"Sure. They paid me to design a few flyers, so I got in on some of the planning of the protest."

"Excellent." Charlie rubbed his hands together. "Well, my dear, I've kept you long enough. I spy the Senior Striders coming around the bend, so I'd best be on my way."

He started out, calmly ignoring the good-natured cat-calls and jeers from the Senior Striders several paces behind him. Jill watched as he tried valiantly to maintain his lead, but before they were out of sight he'd already been swallowed by the pack.

Poor Charlie, she thought as she went back to work. Yet he was certainly better off, trailing the pack or not, than many people his age. His compassion for those less able-bodied endeared him to her. And, though she feared to admit it to herself, she found Spence Jegger's compassion endearing, too.

But she'd let the matter end there. She could share what she knew about the North Dakota shopping center incident. Common decency dictated at least that much. Then she'd move on, as promised. She thought of Spence Jegger's chiseled features, his warm brown eyes, his smile. She'd move on, all right, and fast, if she knew what was good for her.

2

"HIRE HER, Spencer, my boy. She's solid gold, I tell you. She'd be perfect to help you coordinate this protest effort, and if you don't give her a reason to stay longer in Colorado Springs, she'll be gone in a week." Charlie leaned his age-spotted hands on Spence's desk and gazed down at him with fierce intent. "That would be a disaster."

Spence grinned. "Why are you so determined to play matchmaker? I admit she's a good-looking woman, but hardly the only one around. If she's leaving town in a week, I'm sure she has a good reason. Who am I to interfere?"

"You will if you know what's good for you. St. Valentine's Day is exactly—let's see—" Charlie lifted one hand and ticked the days off on his fingers "—fifteen days away."

"So?" Spence tilted his desk chair back.

"Confound it, man! Don't you realize that in your present state of loneliness, you're liable to make a mess of St. Valentine's Day?"

"Who says I'm lonely?"

Charlie pushed himself away from the desk and threw up his hands. "Not I, certainly. I would suppose every eligible man of thirty-two spends his evenings in the back room of his place of business playing chess with an itinerant old bum."

Spence frowned. "I wish you wouldn't call yourself a bum."

"Why not tell the truth? Poverty is nothing to be ashamed of."

"That's right, and being temporarily down on your luck doesn't make you a bum, either."

Charlie scratched his ear. "I'm trying to master the vernacular. I thought that's what the common term was for people like me."

"Not in my book, Charlie. You're obviously well educated, neat as a pin and scrupulously honest. I'd trust you with anything of mine."

"Ah." Charlie rubbed his hands with satisfaction. "Now we're getting somewhere. Will you trust me with your heart?"

"Hey, wait a minute. That's—"

"You said anything," Charlie reminded him. "Now just hear me out. You have a bit of a problem on your hands with Ms Tippy Henderson, correct?"

"You'd better believe it."

"Our Jill has traveled around and spent a great deal of time observing shopping malls, due to her particular line of work. In North Dakota, she gained valuable experience organizing mall tenants into a cohesive unit. You need her expertise."

"And along the way you hope I'll be captured by those green eyes of hers," Spence commented. "You don't fool me with all this concern about the mall problems."

"I most certainly am concerned about the mall problems," Charlie said with an injured glance. "It just so happens that Jill is the answer to your personal problem, as well."

Spence chuckled. "But I don't have a personal problem."

"You're mistaken, my boy. Meet the wrong young woman on February fourteenth, and you'll understand what a momentous problem you have."

"Come off it, Charlie."

"Mark my words," Charlie said, jabbing the air with his forefinger. "In the life of every man and woman there is a significant St. Valentine's Day. I feel quite certain that this one is yours."

"That's because you happen to be here," Spence said, chuckling.

Charlie jumped and eyed him nervously. "What did you mean by that?"

"Naturally you think this will be my big day. You haven't been around to see the others, so you have nothing to compare it with." Spence finished his statement with a wink.

"You've had other significant St. Valentine's Days?"

Spence regarded him with amusement. "Okay, no. I can't remember a single wonderful thing happening on St. Valentine's Day, except when I was five and a beautiful older woman of eight kissed me."

"Ah." Charlie sighed. "That doesn't count. Anyway, this is your year."

Spence decided to humor the old guy to the end of his harangue. "And what, exactly, does that mean?"

"Simply that the first eligible young woman you meet this St. Valentine's Day will be your wife within a year."

Spence threw back his head and laughed. "Wife? Hey, I tried that once, and it didn't work. I don't mind you setting me up with someone for a few dates, but let's not be finding me a wife, okay?"

Charlie sighed. "In this modern age I can expect to be mocked, I suppose. But Spencer, there's a reason your first marriage ended unhappily. That reason will become clear to you in the next month . . . *if* you hire Jill Amory as your adviser for this campaign against Tippy the Lip."

"You're a regular Jeanne Dixon, Charlie, making predictions left and right."

"I suggest this for your own good, my boy. The mall will be a crowded place on St. Valentine's Day. I'd deeply regret seeing you encounter the wrong young lady at this critical juncture."

Spence pushed himself out of his chair. "I don't believe a word of this St. Valentine's baloney, but you've made a good point about Jill's background. And I don't see how an extra week or so will upset her schedule."

Charlie beamed. "Excellent thinking. But try for at least two and a half weeks."

"Charlie, she'll stay as long as she can stay. I can't chain her to the desk."

"I suppose not."

"But you're right about something else," Spence added. "She fascinates me. She's easy to look at, but I'm even more interested in what drives a woman to travel alone all over the country. That takes guts. That's why I bought the window decoration. Pretty I can find without too much trouble, but a spirit of adventure isn't that easy to come by."

Charlie gazed at him. "My instincts are excellent, Spencer. Trust me—she's the one for you." He took out his handkerchief and polished the figure-eight pin on his lapel. "Furthermore, I'm confident that you can persuade her to stay." He glanced up. "And I would pursue the matter immediately, if I were you."

"Yeah, well, why not?" Spence walked around the desk. "Where did you see her last?"

"When the Senior Striders finished up, she was in the vicinity of the Tastefully Lacy lingerie shop."

"Okay." Spence paused and glanced at Charlie's feet. "By the way, did the shoes help?"

"Only my bunions," Charlie said, "not my speed."

"Dead last again, huh?"

"Unfortunately. I don't think Gladys was particularly impressed."

"You might have to consider some serious training, Charlie. Some of those folks have been going at this for two years, and you can't expect to catch up in two months without extra conditioning."

Charlie made a face. "I don't relish charging around the mall during the day by myself. With the Senior Striders, I'm part of a crowd, but alone I might resemble a shoplifter trying to escape capture."

"Train at night," Spence suggested. "Let yourself out the front and take a few turns around the mall when no one is here."

"I've been afraid to venture out alone after the mall closes, in case the security people see me."

"They already know about you, Charlie."

"They do?"

"Sure. Jack and Steve are friends of mine, and besides, they needed to know you're here all night so if a fire breaks out or anything happens, they can rescue you."

"I hadn't thought of that. But, Spencer, they won't tell Tippy the Lip, I hope? I'm certain that my staying here would be against her regulations."

Spence grimaced. "No doubt. That woman decorates her world with red tape. But Jack and Steve won't tell. They don't like her any better than I do. She's already tried to cut their salaries."

"My, my. Where will it end?"

"Who knows, Charlie. I guess my parents were naive to imagine that the same corporation would own the mall forever, but if they'd known what would happen in two short years, they never would've sold the land."

Charlie patted his arm. "You'll put things to rights, my boy. You and Jill Amory."

Spence gazed at the old man and shook his head. "I must be crazy to let you talk me into this. No telling what else you've got up the sleeve of that tweed sport coat."

Charlie merely smiled.

"If she turns out to be some sort of flake, I'm blaming this on you," Spence said, backing out of the office.

"She'll turn out to be wonderful," Charlie replied.

WONDERFUL, Spence repeated to himself as he left the store. He hadn't applied that adjective to a woman in quite a while, not since his courtship days with Gretchen. He still hadn't sorted out whether he'd fallen in love with her or with Germany, and whether she'd fallen for him or his Air Force uniform.

Not that it mattered now. In the end she'd loved Germany more than she'd loved him, and he'd loved Colorado Springs more than he'd loved her. Lots of love, all in the wrong places, couldn't hold their marriage together.

He took the stairs instead of the escalator to the second floor of the mall. Charlie wasn't the only one who wanted to stay in shape, and besides, the wooden stairs with their polished brass railings were too beautiful to be simply ornamental.

Spence would have preferred no escalators at all, because they looked far too modern compared with the wood-and-brass stairways. But some people needed the motorized steps, he realized, and accessibility was a cherished theme in the Remembrance Mall, or at least it had been until Tippy the Lip arrived.

He passed the curtained entrance to the melodrama theater, where the first performance of the morning had begun. Over the mall's piped-in piano music he heard hisses and boos directed at the villain. If the audience only knew, he thought, they'd be hissing and booing in Tippy's office instead. She intended to adopt a "profit-oriented" approach to running the melodrama, and Spence wondered how much longer the show would go on.

He continued down the mall and spotted Jill crouched in front of the lingerie store window, as Charlie had suggested she might be. One correct prediction for Charlie's scorecard, Spence thought, but that was the end of it. St. Valentine's Day or not, Spence wasn't in the market for a wife. He'd welcome someone to laugh and talk with, perhaps, but not someone who'd share a set of monogrammed towels.

In picking out Jill, though, Charlie had shown good taste. Spence admired the dark curls that fell to her shoulders and the lean curve outlined by the seat of her acid-washed jeans. She wore a matching vest today over a bright red blouse the same shade as the paint she applied carefully to the window.

She looked fit, and he always found that sexy. She'd be able to hike into the backwoods and still have energy left over. Spence smiled as he remembered their interview yesterday. Energy left to make love in a double sleeping bag, perhaps.

Of course, the backwoods wasn't exactly inviting in the dead of winter. Jill would have to stay in town until spring for the opportunity to fulfill that particular fantasy. Spence doubted that would happen, considering her apparent determination to finish her trip by June.

By blending in with the crowd of shoppers, Spence was able to approach Jill without her noticing him. He stood about ten feet behind her and watched her work. The creative process intrigued him because he'd never considered himself creative.

Using sure strokes of her brush, Jill dressed a saucy blonde in an ankle-length robe of lace. Spence vaguely remembered the term *peignoir* from his honeymoon with Gretchen. The lace was interspersed with red hearts that conveniently covered everything that would incite the vice squad, but hints of skin color and the suggested outline of a curvaceous body indicated to Spence, at least, that the painted lady was supposed to be naked under the lace.

He swallowed. As if Jill's window decoration weren't suggestive enough, the garments displayed in the showcase unerringly pointed his thoughts in the direction of lust. Filmy things in red and white adorned the mannequins, who all gazed at him with sloe-eyed absorption. He suddenly realized that he'd walked past these windows dozens of times—his favorite cookie shop was two doors away—and never before felt the sensual tug of the merchandise. He had to get a grip on himself.

This was business. He was here to ask Jill if she'd like a job. "Do they sell something like that?" he blurted out, walking up beside her and pointing to the painted lace robe. *Great*, he thought. *I'm sticking to business, all right.*

She glanced up, startled. "Oh . . . hi, Mr. Jegger."

"Hi, Ms Amory," he said, smiling inwardly at the formality, considering Charlie's plans for them. "Nice work."

"Thanks." She stared at him, her brush poised in mid-air.

"Don't drip," he cautioned her as red paint oozed to the tip of the bristles.

She looked at her brush and wiped it against the lip of the paint jar she held in her other hand. "Thanks again."

"Don't let me interrupt," he said when she continued to stand motionless, gazing at him. "The outfit you created with your paint brush is very...uh...nice, and I just wondered if you made it up or if they sell something like that here."

Her glance cooled. "They have these in the shop, if you're interested. They're a special-order item for Valentine's Day, and they asked me to feature them. If you buy one, would you mention that the window art sold you? I like my customers to feel they got their money's worth."

"I'll mention it." He realized that it must sound to her as if he had a girlfriend in mind, when in fact he'd considered buying the garment for Jill. The idea was incredible, of course. He hardly knew her well enough to buy her dinner, let alone a negligee.

The blonde she'd painted on the window looked okay in lace, but Jill's dark hair would be spectacular against the delicate white pattern. He wondered what she'd think if he handed her a box with the robe inside. Once she opened the box she'd probably hand it right back, if she didn't bash him over the head with it first.

"You're doing a great job," he said, sounding like a broken record. "Just keep going. Don't mind me."

"Okay." She dipped the brush in the paint and outlined a heart positioned strategically over one breast. Her hand seemed less steady than before he'd spoken to her, but maybe he was imagining things. "Did you want something in particular?" she asked as she continued to work.

My wants are becoming more particular every moment I'm around you, he thought. "Well, yes, as a matter of fact. Charlie mentioned that you've had some experience with a shopping mall where the tenants organized against the management."

She stopped painting and gave him a wary look. "Charlie doesn't waste much time, does he?"

"No."

"Oh, well. I guess it doesn't matter. I was planning to talk to you about that, anyway. I think it would be a shame for the trolley and motorized carts to become a pay-as-you-go proposition, but you can't expect to fix the problem by yourself. If I were you I'd call a meeting of the other tenants and—"

"Would you help me?" Spence asked, suddenly afraid she'd give him the sum of her advice in a few minutes and drop the matter. "I'll admit my single-handed steamroller approach hasn't worked, but that's the way I operate. I need someone with inventive ideas, and if I could persuade you to stay a little longer than a week, I'd be glad to pay you some sort of retainer."

She didn't respond right away. "Who is Charlie Hartman, exactly?" she asked at last.

He looked into those green eyes of hers and realized that Charlie was definitely right—it would be a crime if Jill left Colorado Springs in a week. "Charlie's a friend of mine who currently lives in the back of my store."

"Is that legal?"

Spence shrugged. "I don't care if it isn't. If Jegger Outfitters were still the only store on this spot, the way it was before Remembrance Mall went up, Charlie's presence would be fine. I'm not going to worry about whether the mall management would want me to offer him a place to stay. I figure the former owners of the land have some rights."

Jill set her jar of paint on the floor and laid the brush across it. "And he's not related to you or anything?" she asked, scratching the tip of her nose.

"Nope. I just like him. He's seems to be—I don't know—someone out of the past or something."

"What about all this matchmaking stuff?"

Spence grinned. "Charlie's old-fashioned in that way, too. He doesn't think a man of my age should be single. He thinks I need a sweetheart."

"Do you?" She glanced at the robe painted on the window. "Or are you keeping secrets from dear old Charlie?"

"I . . . There's no one special," he said, caught without a reasonable explanation for his interest in the robe. "I thought perhaps my mother might—"

She began to laugh. "You won't get away with that one! You can tell me, and I won't even blab to your friend Charlie. Who's the lucky girl?"

"Never mind that," he said impatiently, unwilling to admit the truth and have her laugh even harder. Or maybe she'd be insulted; the robe was pretty sheer. "Let's get back to the mall problem. The thing is, I really do need a temporary adviser, and you seem perfect for the job, if you're at all interested."

Jill folded her arms and sighed. "Well, much as I'd like to stay and help, I can't."

"Why not?" He'd thought he had her, and now she was backing away.

"I can't risk missing my deadline. I left some unfinished business in Maine."

From her tone of voice, he suspected a lover waited for her there. But if that were so, why had she left this guy for a year while she wandered around by herself? He decided to push harder. "I wouldn't keep you here long, I promise."

"With me, any deviation from the plan is dangerous," she said with a wry smile. "I have a reputation for being easily distracted. I've hopped from one thing to another so often that my nickname is Jill of All Trades."

"Does your boyfriend call you that?"

She looked startled. "He's not exactly. . . that is, I . . . Well, anyway. . . yes, Aaron calls me that."

Damn, there was someone. But she obviously wasn't sure about her commitment, so maybe Aaron didn't matter. "You're out to prove you can stick to one thing, painting windows?"

"It's not the windows, it's the trip that's important." She gestured toward the decorated glass. "This won't be my career, if that's what you mean. But Lord knows what will be. I've tried secretarial school, plumbing, appliance sales, small-engine repair—I even considered becoming a concert pianist once. In my one year of college I had four majors, art among them. That's where I picked up the skills to paint windows."

"There's nothing wrong with exploring the job market before you settle down to something," Spence said. He'd been right about her spirit of adventure, he thought. Plumbing? Small-engine repair?

"I agree, but this is ridiculous. I wasn't getting anywhere staying put in Maine, so I decided to see the country and give myself a goal and a deadline. I've never finished anything in my life, unless you count high school. Before I left, I sublet my apartment in Bangor, and I was forced to clean out the evidence of all my

abandoned projects—half-knit sweaters, part of a mac-
ramé hanger, a partially installed whirlpool tub—you get
the idea."

Spence nodded. "I guess so." He wondered how far
along her relationship with this guy Aaron had pro-
gressed. Were they partially in love? Was that condition
possible?

"I'm petrified of getting off track and not completing
this trip on time. I have to prove to myself that I can do
it. You might not understand. You look like a man who's
always known what he wanted."

"I don't know where you got that idea." Spence gazed
at her and realized his wants were changing by the second.

"You're working in your family business, and it obviously suits you. As for me, I don't know where I fit."

Perhaps with me, came the silent reply, but Spence
pushed it away. "How do you know Colorado Springs
isn't the place to find an answer?" he said, choosing a
more oblique response.

She gave him a long considering glance. "It might be,
but I still have to stay on schedule and complete this trip.
I promised myself." She smiled fondly. "And someone
else."

His heart sank. "Aaron?"

"No, not Aaron. My great-grandmother. G.G. She's
the only one back home who continues to have faith in
me. She believes I'll finish this trip, and she bought a
scrapbook to paste postcards in from every state capital. I can't disappoint an eighty-two-year-old woman
with a scrapbook to fill, can I?"

"But just a few days wouldn't—"

"With me, it could. I know myself. I'm sorry. But I'll be glad to tell you how the North Dakota deal went." She bent to pick up her paint and brush, as if dismissing him.

"Wait a minute." He heard the sharp edge to his words but couldn't help himself. "You really can't see taking a few extra days for a good cause? I'm talking about old folks and handicapped people, and preserving some history, and—"

"I realize all that," she interrupted, turning back to him. "I've been a sucker for good causes all my life, but this time I can't be."

Spence was growing more irritated by the minute. "Isn't that a tad selfish?" And Charlie thought this person was right for him? Fat chance.

"Call it what you will," she said, and resumed her painting.

"I call it self-absorbed," he said, and felt some satisfaction when she winced at the criticism. "Well, see you on Friday."

"Aren't you going to buy that lacy thing for your girlfriend before you leave?" she taunted without looking up.

"No." He spun on his heel and walked away.

"Better not wait too long," she called after him. "Valentine's Day is just around the corner."

He turned back to make some sarcastic retort, but thought better of it. He was acting ridiculous, letting her get to him like this. Maybe he'd actually believed Charlie's garbage about how wonderful she was, and now he was like a kid disappointed at Christmas by the wrong gift. He slapped his thigh in frustration and headed back for the store.

Charlie was waiting when he returned. Spence closed the office door and related what had happened while the wrinkles in Charlie's face sagged into an expression of gloom.

"This is terrible, my boy," Charlie said when Spence finished talking. "But she'll come around. With a name like Amory she can't be so hardened to the plight of others."

"So you say. I say forget Jill Amory."

"I can't have been wrong about her."

"No? And what about this boyfriend she has stashed in Maine?"

"Look at the facts, Spencer, my boy. She left him to travel the country for an entire year. Does that sound like a viable relationship?"

"At this point, I don't care."

Charlie left his chair to pace the room. "I could check the files on this Aaron situation, of course," he muttered, "but the filing system isn't what it should be on these matters, and I usually find that—"

"What filing system?" Spence leaned forward on his desk and gazed at Charlie in consternation. "Charlie, what on earth . . . ?"

"Nothing," Charlie said quickly. "You know old people. They talk to themselves a great deal of the time about inconsequentials."

"What was all that about checking files on people?"

"Files? I must have meant smiles. I base many of my judgments on smiles, don't you? Jill Amory has a wonderful smile, don't you agree?"

"I couldn't say. She wasn't using it much when I last saw her."

"I can see we have a minor setback here," Charlie observed. "But I'm sure I can put things to rights. Plan A didn't work, so I'll concoct Plan B."

"Charlie, forget this, okay?" Spence grew uneasy as he watched the old man stroke his chin and pace the length of his office.

"I'm still thinking. I wonder if . . . hmm . . . aha!"

"What?"

"Never mind, Spencer, my boy. Leave everything to me."

"No, really, I—"

"I'll be back," Charlie said, heading out the door of Spence's office. "I have people to see."

"Charlie—"

Charlie poked his head back in the door. "Trust me," he whispered and left.

3

JILL WASN'T SURPRISED when Charlie showed up again later in the morning. She'd nearly finished the shoe store window, which featured one high-heeled sandal facing a man's black dress oxford. She'd added eyes and mouths to both shoes and was outlining the conversation bubble that came from the red-lipped mouth at the toe of the sandal.

"My, but you are clever," Charlie remarked, sticking his thumb in his vest while he gazed at the window. "Anthropomorphic footwear."

Jill sorted through her vocabulary. "Making something human that's not, right?"

"Exactly. Now perhaps I can guess the slogan you'll use. Is it *I'll love you heart and sole, Valentine*?"

"That's close." Jill chuckled. "I thought maybe I'd use *Let's be solemates, Valentine*."

"I like that better," Charlie said.

"Oh, why?"

"Because it's a briefer message," he said in that cultured accent Jill couldn't identify. "When you finish this window, may I suggest a lunch break?"

Jill smiled and began her lettering inside the bubble. The old guy was so transparent—he wanted to spend the lunch hour convincing her to take Spence's offer. And unfortunately for her determination to finish the trip, she was already weakening. Spence's comments about selfishly pursuing her own goals had struck a nerve. "How do you know I haven't eaten lunch?" she asked, giving an extra flourish to the first *s* in *solemates*.

"I've been checking on you between errands."

She had to admire his dedication. "Charlie, it's no good. I'd like to stay and help the cause, but I can't afford the risk to my plan." She sounded selfish even to herself now, but she plunged on. "When I finish painting all the windows I've contracted for in this mall, I'll hit the road for Salt Lake City." She finished the lettering and swirled her brush in a jar of water. "I want to get through Utah and on to California in plenty of time to paint Easter windows there."

"I see." Charlie took out his handkerchief and polished his gold figure-eight pin. "Well, all that aside, I would be so very honored if you'd join me at one of the fast-food eateries downstairs."

"You won't be able to change my mind, Charlie," Jill warned, although she was no longer sure that was true.

"I understand perfectly," he replied, folding his handkerchief neatly and returning it to his pocket.

"And we're going Dutch," Jill added. From the worn places on Charlie's clothes, she'd deduced that he didn't have much spare cash.

"Dutch? I don't believe they have any fast-food restaurants featuring dishes from Holland. I thought perhaps we'd try the place that serves hot dogs on a stick. I believe they're called corndogs, but that doesn't sound Dutch to me."

"You don't know what going Dutch means?"

Charlie frowned in confusion. "Judging from your question, apparently not."

"It means I'll pay for my hot dog and you'll pay for yours. Dutch treat."

"Why on earth would it be called that?"

"I don't know, Charlie." Jill stored her paints and picked up the carrying case. "But I can't imagine you've never heard the expression. Where have you been hanging out, anyway?"

"Nowhere, I hope," Charlie said, glancing down at his clothes. "Although perhaps some of these seams may be coming apart," he added, straining to see over his shoulder. "I—"

"Never mind, Charlie," Jill said, taking his arm. "Nothing's ripped. Let's go eat." She started walking down the mall. "Stairs or escalator?"

"Stairs. I have the worst time deciding which of those rolling steps to take. Lines form behind me while I work up my courage to stand on one and let it carry me down. Once a large man picked me up and deposited me on the step in front of him. I was dreadfully embarrassed and haven't ridden the escalator since."

"Makes sense," Jill said. "I've never been wild about them, either." In spite of herself, Jill was growing fond of Charlie. Maybe she was homesick, she thought, and Charlie reminded her of G.G.

She considered whether she ought to call Aaron tonight, although she tried to keep long-distance expenses to a minimum. Besides that, whenever she called she could hear the unspoken question from him: Have you settled on what to do with your life so you can give up this crazy trip and come home? Unfortunately, the answer was still no.

"Spencer filled me in on your conversation with him this morning," Charlie said when they'd bought their corndog lunch and seated themselves in an orange plastic booth. "And I admire your dedication to your goal."

"Your friend Mr. Jegger thinks I'm selfish."

"Spencer is a bit quick on the trigger. I'm sure you're not selfish. You have a sense of commitment. Besides, I understand your great-grandmother expects a postcard from every state capital."

"That's right. She's expecting one from Salt Lake City in about ten days."

"Ten days." Charlie clucked his tongue. "Far too soon. I can't believe that your great-grandmother would want you to turn your back on true love," he added slyly.

"Charlie, you said you weren't going to do this."

Charlie shook his corndog at her. "But Spencer is such a wonderful—"

"Then I could drive back to Colorado Springs this summer, couldn't I? Maybe I agree with you. He seems like a really nice guy, and maybe I should get to know him. But first I have to finish this trip."

"You don't understand," Charlie said, gesturing more wildly with his corndog. "Valentine's Day is crucial. That's the time when Spencer, and perhaps you, as well, will suddenly— Oh, my gracious!"

Jill watched his corndog sail from the stick and arc over his shoulder. Charlie twisted in the booth and winced as the corndog landed with a plop on the table behind them.

"Mommy, somebody's corndog flew over here!" shouted a little boy of about five.

Jill smothered her laughter with her hand as the little boy grabbed the half-eaten corndog and scrambled to his knees facing Charlie.

"Mister?" he said, shoving the corndog forward. "Did you lose this?"

"Why, yes, I believe I did," Charlie replied gravely, and accepted the corndog as if it were a gold pocket watch. "Thank you for retrieving it, young man."

"You're welcome," the little boy said, equally solemn. "Sometimes food gets away from me, too."

Jill glanced into the merry face of the little boy's mother, who was also having trouble controlling herself. The two women exchanged a glance of shared fun before returning their attention to their lunch companions.

"I thought they were more firmly attached," Charlie said as he skewered his meal with the wooden stick. "Now, where were we?" he asked, wiping his fingers on a napkin.

"I'm going to miss you when I leave here, Charlie," Jill said with a smile.

"I'm not important. Your future is. Which reminds me of what I was saying. Aren't you aware of the legend of St. Valentine's Day?"

Jill sipped her drink. "I guess not."

"Well, when conditions are propitious, meaning that a man or woman is ready to find a mate for life, he or she will marry the first eligible person they meet on St. Valentine's Day, and the wedding will take place within a year."

"You say that so seriously, Charlie, as if you really believe it."

Charlie gazed at the ceiling. "Forgive them their ignorance. They're children of the modern age."

"Charlie, come on! That's superstition and you know it."

"I certainly do not know it. And if Spencer doesn't meet a suitable young woman on February fourteenth, there's no telling who he might end up with. I feel an overwhelming responsibility, knowing that he'll be here in the mall that day, among crowds of female prospects.

Why, he could run into almost anyone. It's frightening. That's why you simply must stay."

Jill was trying hard not to giggle. Charlie's eccentricity was laughable, but touching, too, in a way. She couldn't bear to make fun of him and hurt his feelings. "Work on another girl," she suggested. "I won't be here on February fourteenth. I have to finish my trip so I can point to that accomplishment whenever I'm accused of not finishing what I start."

"Spencer mentioned your nickname."

"Jill of All Trades, Mistress of None."

Charlie clucked in disapproval. "Negative messages, negative messages," he said. "How I despise them."

"People have reason to say that about me," Jill admitted after taking a swallow of lemonade. "That's why I'm so determined . . ." She lost her train of thought, distracted by the woman and her little boy leaving the booth.

"You must not intend to be a window painter, then." Charlie searched through their lunch bag for another container of mustard. "Although I can't imagine why not, with your obvious talent and cleverness."

Jill didn't answer as she concentrated on the mother and child. She watched until they were out of sight.

"What is it?" Charlie asked.

"Nothing. What were you saying?" Jill glanced back at him and smiled.

"We were discussing your career."

"Oh, that. Well, I want a career where I can make a difference in the world. That much I do know. I've had fun painting windows, but it's a means to an end, a way to buy thinking time and discover what I really should do."

"Hmm."

"People have told me I can do anything I set my mind to, so I guess the reason I never finish anything is that I haven't set my mind to it."

"Except you've finished painting windows all over the country."

"That doesn't count." Jill had her corndog halfway to her mouth for another bite when three older men sauntered into the restaurant and glanced around as if looking for someone.

"There he is," said one, a plump fellow with glasses who then led the way back to their booth. "Hey, Charlie!"

Charlie turned in his seat. "Robert! And Bernie and George, too. Glad you could make it."

"When something's important, it's important," the man in glasses said as he slid in beside Charlie.

Charlie nodded. "Right you are. Jill, I'd like you to meet some friends of mine from the Senior Striders," he continued. "This is Robert, and over there's Bernie."

"Hi." Jill made room for a gaunt man who leaned a hickory walking stick against the wall before sitting down. She knew Charlie was up to something, but she was also curious enough to stay around for a little while and find out what it was.

"And that's George." Charlie motioned to the ruddy-faced, balding man pulling a chair up to the end of the table. "Gentleman, I'd like you to meet Jill Amory, the lady who's been creating the clever valentine window painting."

"Excellent job, young woman," George said from the end of the table. "And I see you even consented to have lunch with this old coot."

"Yes, but she insisted on a Holland treat," Charlie grumbled.

Jill glanced at the puzzled expressions surrounding her and bit her lip to keep from laughing. "Um, that's Dutch treat, Charlie."

"Oh," Robert said with a relieved chuckle. "Dutch treat. I get it. Dutch . . . Holland. Sometimes I think Charlie's been on another planet for the past fifty years, you know?"

Smiling, Jill nodded.

"Whether I understand all the idioms of the modern day is unimportant," Charlie said testily. "We're here to discuss the mall problems."

"Just as I suspected, Charlie," Jill said, realizing he'd called these men in as reinforcements. "This is one meeting I won't be attending. I have work to do, so if you'll please let me by, Bernie, I'll leave you gentlemen to your discussion."

Bernie started to rise. "I was afraid of this, Charlie. Maybe this mall situation will end up being my job, after all."

"Don't be hasty, my good man," Charlie said. "You remember what we decided about that."

"Right," added Robert. "Sit down a second, Bern," he directed.

Jill didn't understand their cryptic comments, nor did she want to. "Listen, I—"

Robert leaned toward her. "Can you give us five minutes of your time? That's all we ask. Five minutes. You haven't finished your lunch, so you can eat while we talk."

"I can take this with me," she said, picking up her corndog and drink to demonstrate how easily she could leave, lunch and all.

"We have new information about the scope of the problem," George added. "And if what Charlie says about your character is true, you'll want to hear this."

Jill glanced at Charlie. "My character?"

"Charlie's an excellent judge of character," Bernie said, turning toward her. "He thinks highly of you, so we've agreed to this meeting as a way of convincing you to help us."

"Just give us five minutes," Robert repeated.

"Whatever Charlie told you, I'm not worth all this attention," Jill said, laughing.

"We'll be the judge of that," George said. "Can we tell you what we've found out?"

"I guess so." With a resigned sigh she put her food back on the table. To be honest, having these men court her for her experience felt good.

"You first, Robert," George said.

"Well, it looks like the melodrama theater's done for," Robert said, taking off his glasses and reaching for a napkin from the dispenser. "Word has it that the amateur groups will be charged a hefty fee for performing starting next week." Robert breathed on his lenses and polished them with the napkin. "I'd underwrite the costs myself, but I've heard Tippy really wants to convert the space back to retail." After his speech Robert replaced his glasses and peered through them at Jill.

"Tippy's hoping to evict the museum, too, and get a department store chain to lease that space," added Bernie.

"Has anyone besides Spence Jegger talked with her?" Jill asked.

"Gladys tried," George said. "Tippy warned her that the Senior Striders were on shaky ground anyway, because their exercise program took space on the walkways and might interfere with other people who were there to spend money."

"The woman does sound like a barracuda," Jill acknowledged.

"And she's moving fast," Charlie added, shaking his head. "Something must be done at once."

"A protest of the tenants is the only way to approach this," George said from the end of the table. "She'd have to pay attention to them. With Spencer at the helm and a good assistant, which we hope will be you, we'd have a chance to turn the situation around."

Jill put down her naked corndog stick. "I'm sure Spence can handle it without me." She could feel herself rapidly losing her conviction, thinking maybe a few extra days would do the trick. Then she'd push on to Salt Lake City.

"Spencer's taking inventory at the store. Everyone in the mall does at this time of year," George said. "Unfortunately, I don't think we can let this problem go until after inventory."

"I'll help in any way I can," Robert said, "but I haven't met all the tenants. Charlie pointed out that Jill has, and recently, through her window-painting business. We also need someone with clerical skills, which I don't have. I always hired secretaries to do that when I was in business."

"Same here," George said.

"We need someone young and energetic, someone with creative ideas," Bernie added, turning to her. "You seem perfect for the job."

Jill leaned back against the unyielding plastic booth and focused on Charlie. "You wouldn't call this heavy-handed or anything, would you?"

"My dear, I simply feel that you need to be fully aware of the situation. Perhaps if you could see your way clear to give us three weeks . . ." He lifted his bushy gray eyebrows in silent appeal.

"For the good of the mall, or because you want me to fall in love with Spence Jegger?" she said boldly.

Robert looked startled. "Fall in love? Who said anything about falling in love?"

Jill could tell from the flush on Charlie's lined cheeks that he hadn't mentioned that aspect to his Senior Strider buddies.

"Yeah, Charlie," George said, leaning forward. "I thought you wanted us to convince Jill to stay and help, but you didn't say anything about matchmaking."

Charlie turned a deeper shade of red. "Well, I . . ."

"He's a romantic, that's all," Jill said, taking pity on Charlie. "And maybe he did think Mr. Jegger and I might get together, but that's not the important issue, really. Right, Charlie?"

"Of course it's not," Bernie said. "But I can see why Charlie might pick up that idea, along with the other. You and Spence would make a fine-looking couple."

"But that's strictly their business," George said, looking ruddier than ever. "Strictly their business."

"I'm glad to hear it," Jill said, "because this is what I've decided to do. My work will keep me here a few more days, and I'm willing to devote any spare time to this project. When the windows are finished, I will stay for a reasonable length of time and work full-time on the problem, for whatever that's worth. Maybe it'll be worth nothing, and whether we've solved the problem or not, I'll have to leave."

"How long would that be, exactly?" Charlie asked.

She looked him straight in the eye. "About ten days, maximum."

Charlie flinched. "But—"

"Hey," Robert said, warding off the protest, "that's better than nothing. We might have this problem wrapped up by then."

"All right." Charlie sighed. "Have you a moment to go tell Spencer the news before you return to your painting?"

"I'm not sure he'll be pleased to hear it. We didn't part on very friendly terms."

"He'll be glad," Charlie said. "Please do drop by the store for a moment."

"Okay. Or rather, I will if you gentlemen are ready to set me loose. I feel a little like a hostage."

"I'm sorry if we strong-armed this through," George said, moving his chair so Bernie could slide out of the booth. "But Charlie convinced us you were the one for the job, and we were determined to convince you."

"Which I guess we did," Robert added with a satisfied smile.

"You all made some good points," Jill said, "but they weren't the real clinchers for me."

"What was, pray tell?" Charlie asked.

"The mother of the little boy who returned your corndog. You had your back turned when they left, but she walked out of here on crutches. I don't know if she'll be making enough purchases to buy a place on that trolley, but she shouldn't have to. I'd like to help, if I can."

"Bravo, my dear," Charlie said, beaming. "Bravo."

"Thank you, young lady," Bernie said, shaking her hand. "We'll be standing by. Just tell us what to do. We're all poor typists, as we've said, but there must be some jobs we can accomplish."

"Mr. Jegger will probably let you know," Jill said, also pausing to shake Robert's and George's hands.

"Are you certain you won't consider an extra week?" Charlie asked again.

"Charlie, leave the poor woman alone," Robert cautioned. "We'll get the job done in the time she has, that's all."

"I fear that I won't," Charlie said. "I mean, *we* won't," he amended hastily. "Even another five days would be helpful."

Jill gazed at him and smiled. "I have my goals, too, Charlie," she said. "And I intend to achieve them. I'll talk with you all soon." Then she turned and left the restaurant.

JEGGER'S OUTFITTERS was only a short distance from the food court. Carrying her case of paint supplies, Jill walked through the door and glanced around. Between the open shelves she could see Spence near the back of the store with a customer. He was explaining something about tents, judging from the way he gestured to various models set up in that area.

Jill wondered how he'd react after their last heated conversation, and how he'd interpret her decision to stay an extra few days. She'd simply tell him that she'd decided to do it for the good of all, in the name of what was right and decent in the world. That was the truth, as far as it went, and he might believe her. Then again, he might notice the slight tremor of her hand, or the quickening of her breath when she was around him. If he noticed, he might guess that her motives weren't as pure as she tried to convince herself they were.

Her plan to leave in ten days meant she'd be gone before Valentine's Day, which would tell him that she wasn't catering to this nonsense about love and fate. But in reality Charlie's predictions about love and marriage made her nervous. She'd run away from one commitment in Maine because she wasn't ready. And she still wasn't.

She waited until Spence had helped the customer carry a large box to the checkout counter. There the young clerk, Horace, stood ready to ring up the tent purchase. When Spence started walking back to his office, she hurried forward and called his name.

He turned, looking confused when he saw her. "You're not ready for the windows, are you?" he asked, coming toward her. "I thought it would be at least tomorrow."

"It will. That's not why I'm here. I talked with Charlie, and decided to stay on a few days beyond what I'd originally planned. If you could use my services, I'll be in town another seven to ten days."

He leaned one hand against a rough shelf and gazed at her. "I'm sorry about what I said."

"It's okay. I probably deserved it."

"Obviously not. You're staying."

"Just a few days," she cautioned.

He raised an eyebrow. "Not through February fourteenth?"

"Nope."

"I have the feeling Charlie unloaded his St. Valentine's Day theory on you."

"He did," Jill admitted, heart thumping.

"And you don't care to stick around and test it." His smile gently teased her.

"It really wouldn't matter if I stayed longer or not. All this significance Charlie attaches to Valentine's Day is silly, don't you think?"

"Of course it is." His brown eyes glowed with good humor.

"Of course," she echoed.

"So why run away?"

"I'm not running," she said, her mouth dry. "I've told you what my schedule is. And I may be foolish to spend any extra time here, but it's a good cause, and I think I can help. However, if you don't want to accept my offer..."

"No. I'm grateful for whatever days you can spare. How about dinner? We can discuss the particulars then."

Jill glanced at her watch. "If you don't mind, I'd rather grab a hamburger and eat while I work. We can talk after the mall closes, so I won't lose potential working time."

"Sounds reasonable. We can meet here a few minutes before nine."

"I'll be here. See you then." She turned to go.

"Jill." He spoke her name softly. It was the first time he'd used her given name, she realized.

"Yes?"

"Thanks."

"Don't thank me yet, Spence," she said, trying out his first name, liking the sound of it. "We haven't even started."

His slow smile quietly contradicted her.

Heart racing, she turned and hurried out of the store.

4

JILL DESCENDED the oak staircase listening to the familiar echoing sounds of closing time: the soft thunder of metal grid doors sliding down over store entrances; the clack of long-handled dustpans; the bump of wheeled buckets rolling over the imitation brick flooring.

But unlike other malls where Jill had worked, here there was also the clang of a trolley bell as the conductor finished his last run, and the laughter of an audience filing out of the melodrama after the last performance. No doubt about it, the atmosphere of Remembrance Mall was special, and Jill was willing to spend time to help preserve its unique character.

The question was, how dangerous to her plans was this liaison with Spence? She remembered one of G.G.'s favorite sayings—that obstacles in your path test whether you want something or just think you do. Spence Jegger was the biggest obstacle she had encountered on her path so far. Spence and Charlie, she amended.

She arrived at the entrance to Jegger's Outfitters and ducked under the metal door that had been left partially open. An athletic-looking young woman of about eighteen was closing out the cash register.

"Is Spence around?" Jill asked, glancing toward the back office.

"He and Charlie are in the storeroom," the girl said. "Are you Jill?"

"Yep."

"He said to send you back. It's through that curtain."

Jill followed the girl's directions into an unfinished area of exposed studs and shiny insulation. Rows of steel shelving lined up library-style held stacks of boxes. To her right, from behind a barrier of shelving she heard men's voices. "Spence?" she called out.

"Hey, Jill!" he called back, and appeared around the end of the shelving. "Come and see Charlie's apartment."

When she arrived at the makeshift doorway, she laughed with delight. "This is terrific, Charlie."

"I should say so." Charlie, his tweed coat off and his red vest unbuttoned, stretched his arms in both directions. "Welcome to my domicile. I worry that Spencer requires this space for storage, but he's assured me that he doesn't."

Jill glanced at Spence, who was leaning against the metal shelving. She'd have a tough time resisting a guy who provided a poor old man with such a comfortable place to live.

One side of the long, narrow space contained a small iron bedstead, neatly made up with blankets pulled so tight a quarter would have bounced on them. Next to the bed were wooden shelves that held a hotplate, dishes and a two-foot-square refrigerator. Opposite was a faded easy chair with an unmatched ottoman and an end table that held several books and a chess set with a game in progress. A framed poster of a red rose lying across piano keys hung from an exposed stud on the wall, and through a partially closed door Jill glimpsed the bathroom. Everything looked neat as a military barracks before inspection.

"Come and sit down, my dear," Charlie said, taking her elbow and guiding her toward the easy chair. "You've had a long day."

"But this is your chair," she protested not very convincingly. She sighed in relief as she sank into it.

"Put your feet up," he added. "Let me take your things."

Jill relinquished her box of painting supplies and her coat before resting her feet on the ottoman. On her own for so long, she'd almost forgotten the luxury of having someone else to care for her. She'd been on her feet for hours, but she hadn't noticed her fatigue until she sat down. "This is a wonderful chair," she said, glancing at Spence.

"Used to be my dad's," he said, watching her with a tender expression. "He had a fit when my mom said it was too shabby for the living room. Instead of hauling it to the dump, he brought it to the store. Now that they're retired, he doesn't get down here to sit much, but Charlie's making use of it."

"Then all this was here before?"

"Everything except the bed and the poster. Oh, and the chess set. That's Charlie's."

Jill looked at the board. "And I interrupted your game."

"That's just as well, my dear." Charlie perched on the edge of the bed. "Spencer had me on the ropes, as usual."

"Don't let him kid you. Charlie's the chess champion of the Remembrance Mall, and I lose more games than I win." Spence's voice held a note of affection. "Anyway, now that you're here, I'll close up the front of the store and make sure Stephanie's got everything under control. Be right back."

After he left, Jill turned to Charlie. "Do you and Spence play chess a lot?"

"Not really. He doesn't have the time. But the game serves as a diversion at quitting time," Charlie explained. "He likes to give Stephanie or Horace, whoever's closing up shop, a chance to tally the receipts without hanging over their shoulder. He wants to build confidence in those young people."

Jill nodded. "That's a good idea."

"Spencer is a wonderful man, Jill. Did you know he was named for one of the great philanthropists in Colorado Springs's history?"

"No, I didn't."

"Spencer Penrose was the fellow's name." Charlie reached under his bed and took a book from a neat stack. "And our Spencer's middle name is Penrose. I've been reading about Mr. Penrose's contributions, and there's a lengthy list—the Pikes Peak Highway, the Broadmoor Hotel, the Cheyenne Mountain Zoo—all sorts of valuable things."

"I have a feeling you're leading up to something, Charlie."

"Only that our Spencer's ideals and community spirit reflect well upon his predecessor. And the most wonderful part of the story is that Spencer Penrose was encouraged in all of this by his talented and creative wife, Julie."

Jill leaned her head against the back of the chair. "You are such a romantic, Charlie."

"Well, of course I am. What other posture makes sense in this world, I ask you?"

"You may have a point."

"I also noticed," Charlie said, closing the book, "how similar your name is to Mrs. Penrose's name. Spencer and Julie. Spencer and Jill. Both combinations sound rather nice, wouldn't you say?"

"I would say that I've never met such a determined matchmaker in my life." She closed her eyes to rest them.

"Couldn't you possibly stay until February fourteenth?"

"No, Charlie," she said without opening her eyes. She heard his sigh of defeat and smiled. "If Spence Jegger and I are right for each other, we'll know before February fourteenth."

"I think so, too," Spence said from the doorway.

Jill's eyes flew open and heat rose to her cheeks as she stared across the little room at him. "I . . . didn't expect you back so soon."

Spence smiled at her. "Stephanie's efficient."

"Why don't I leave you two alone to talk?" Charlie said quickly, moving toward the door. "I can take my evening exercise. Is the key in the usual place?"

"Sure is."

"Then I'll be on my way." With a satisfied expression on his face, Charlie left the storeroom.

"Where's he going?" Jill asked, sitting up straighter and putting her feet on the floor.

"For a walk in the mall. He knows where I keep the key, so he lets himself out through the metal sliding door, relocks it and comes back the same way." Spence crossed to the ottoman and sat on it. His knees were only a few inches from hers.

"Oh."

"I guess we'd better get to work, although I feel a little guilty about loading more on you. You seemed pretty tired when you came in here."

"That's okay. I'm not tired anymore," she stammered, unnerved by his closeness.

He leaned his forearms on his knees and gazed at her. "Actually, you don't look tired now. You look scared to death."

"Nonsense."

"Hey, I won't bite. And if it makes you feel any better, the security guards started their rounds five minutes ago. You can scream and they'll come and whack me over the head with night sticks until you tell them to stop."

She laughed and felt better. "It's just that we've never been alone together, and with all Charlie's talk about romance, I'm nervous. Charlie's really done a number on us. I'm not interested in a relationship, Spence. I could have had that by staying in Maine, but I hardly felt ready to commit myself to a man when my whole future was a question mark."

"I understand. And if it makes you feel any better, I'm not in the market for a relationship, either."

"Oh. Good," she said, feeling deflated by this unexpected announcement. Reluctance on her part was okay, but reluctance on his challenged her ego. "Why not?"

"I was burned not too long ago. I was so sure that we were both ready for marriage." He shrugged. "Obviously we weren't. The divorce became final last November."

"I see." So he'd been married. Jill wasn't crazy about this information, either.

"I need a vacation from involvement, as I told Charlie," Spence added.

"What did he say to that?"

"He just smiled his wise little smile and told me I didn't know what I was talking about."

"Well, we both know about Charlie," Jill said, trying for lightness to salvage her ego. "He's as sweet and nutty as my great-grandmother's fruitcake."

"He's been fun to have around, though."

"I'll bet. I already know he's one of the people I'll want to keep in touch with them when I go back to Maine."

"Have you met very many people like that?"

She glanced at him, gratified by the interest his question revealed. "A few."

"Guys?"

"Why?" she challenged, feeling better by the minute.

"Just . . . a little curious."

"Mmm."

"Okay, dammit, a lot curious."

"I thought you didn't want to get involved?" She couldn't resist putting a point on it.

"I don't, but—"

"Okay. Let's stop playing games. Eight months ago Aaron Fielding asked me to be his wife. I told him I wasn't ready to be anybody's wife until I found some direction in my life. Then I started this trip. I've met some nice guys along the way, but I haven't allowed any romances to develop, because I'd have to give the same answer I gave Aaron, and Aaron asked me first."

"Do you think you'll go back to him?"

"I'll go back to give my answer. Whether I say yes or no to his proposal, I have to tell him in person. That's only fair."

"Do you know your answer?"

"What does it matter to you?" Her heart was beating swiftly in response to the chances they were taking in this conversation. "You said you aren't interested in a relationship with me." *And it isn't true*, she thought, looking into his eyes.

He rubbed his chin and gazed at her. "The more I'm around you, the more I forget that I'm not interested in a relationship," he admitted.

Her insides quivered. She had to stop this. Didn't she? "You were negligee shopping today. Who for?"

"And why would you care?" he countered with a smile. "You're not interested in a relationship with me."

"I've confided in you about Aaron. You can at least tell me who the nightgown is for."

"If I tell you, you won't believe me," he said.

"I might."

He took a deep breath. "I honestly thought about buying it for you."

Jill flopped back in the chair and stared up at the shiny insulation in the ceiling. "We have big trouble here."

"That depends."

She brought her gaze back to him. "Did you buy it?"

"No. I figured you wouldn't accept it from me."

She rubbed the worn arms of the chair and looked away from his tempting brown eyes, his slightly parted lips. "You're right, I wouldn't have. Couldn't. I've promised myself that I— Anyway, aren't we getting sidetracked? We're supposed to be discussing the mall."

"All right. Let's discuss the mall," he said easily. "We have to do that eventually, anyway."

She glanced away from the knowing gleam in his eyes. He could afford to be a little patient, and he knew it. "Got something I can write on?"

"I think so." Spence leaned down to peer under the bed. "I gave Charlie a few legal pads. The guy's a self-made scholar, I guess. He's always reading and taking notes. Yeah, here's an unused one." He pulled the yellow pad of paper from under the bed and dusted it off. Then he took a ballpoint pen from the pocket of his shirt and handed the pen and paper to Jill. "Where do we start?"

She tried to ignore the inner turmoil caused by his hand brushing her knee. "I've had time to think about this while I was painting, and I'd suggest a meeting of the tenants as soon as possible." She rested the pad across her tingling knee. "Find out where we stand."

"I agree."

"If we delivered flyers tomorrow, the meeting could take place the following night. Then you'd know how many are in your camp, and who would be willing to put pressure on the management to keep the mall the way it is." The scent of his after-shave was driving her crazy. She might have known he'd wear something she liked.

He nodded. "Good. We can set the meeting for seven. Most everyone can leave their clerks in charge for an hour or two. Can you spare the time then?"

"Day after tomorrow?" She struggled to concentrate on the business at hand. "I should be finished with the windows by then, and sure, I can be there. I'll design the flyers before I leave tonight and you can have them run off at the photocopying shop." She scribbled a note about the time of the meeting. "It'll be handy, having so many conveniences right here. The mall reminds me of a small town, in a way."

"That's what Charlie says. According to him, the concept of a shopping mall gave him a whole new lease on life. It's almost as if he didn't realize they existed until now. How could he not know that?"

"Charlie seems to have missed lots of things," Jill said, doodling on the edge of the pad. "He's either eccentric or senile." She laughed nervously. "Or someone from another planet. Maybe all those science fiction stories about aliens are true."

"If so, Charlie would be from Venus, with all his talk about love."

Her gaze was drawn to his, the word *love* sitting between them like a dimpled Cupid demanding attention.

Jill glanced at her doodles and realized they were hearts with arrows through them. She'd been painting too many valentine messages recently. "Where shall we hold the meeting?" she asked, making cross-hatch marks over the hearts until they were obliterated.

"We can use the museum." Spence massaged the back of his neck. "Damn, I hope people support this. Tippy's promised increased revenue and lower rents. I'm willing to pay a little more in rent to support the museum and the trolley, but I can't vouch for the others, and friendly persuasion has never been my long suit. I get impatient if people don't immediately see what I want them to see."

Jill smiled. "Like today, when I wouldn't take your job offer?"

"Like today. Charlie's persistence is what got you here. Incidentally, I will pay you for this. We never agreed on an amount, or whether you'd like an hourly wage or a flat fee."

"To tell the truth, I'd like my wages in merchandise. My Coleman stove's about had it, and I noticed a few other supplies out there I could use."

"Don't tell me you're camping across the country?"

"Sort of. Whenever I can find something like a KOA campground."

He looked skeptical. "Out of necessity, or do you like doing that?"

"Out of necessity, but I do like it. Traveling light—in fact, just plain traveling—has been fun, and the camping has been a great adventure."

"No kidding. You really are a kindred spirit," he said, admiration reflected in his eyes. "I wonder if old Charlie's on to something, after all."

"Lots of women like to camp." Her heart began thumping in her chest.

"Not with the self-sufficiency you're demonstrating, they don't."

The fatigue from the day, the stimulation of his nearness and the warmth of his praise were dissolving her restraint. If she sat in the chair much longer, she'd let him kiss her. And from the look in his eyes she thought he might try. "You haven't said whether or not I can take camping supplies in payment," she prompted.

"What? Oh, sure. That's fine." He continued to gaze at her. "Don't you get cold? Or scared being on your own like that?"

"I...sure, sometimes, on both counts. But I've learned how to dress warmly for the cold nights, and I'm braver than I used to be. The trip's been good for me, for my self-confidence." She watched the glow of affection in his eyes grow brighter. He was definitely planning to kiss her. It seemed the more she talked about herself, the more he liked what he heard.

And the longer she sat in Charlie's soft chair, the more she wanted to be held and kissed. She might have developed self-sufficiency in the past seven months, but that didn't mean she was impervious to the lure of a caring man's strong arms. At this moment she wanted to be cuddled, just for a little while.

It wouldn't be just for a little while, though, and she knew it. She had to resist the lethargy that was overtaking her and assert her independence, or she'd be lost. She put the legal pad and pen on the table beside her. "Let's go out in front and I'll show you what I'd like in exchange for my work," she suggested.

He looked amused. "All right," he said, standing up and leading the way out of Charlie's intimate little nest. "Last I heard they were predicting snow for tonight," he commented, as if to remind her of the realities of her temporary life-style.

Jill chuckled. "Then maybe I'd better take an advance on my pay in the form of some red long johns."

He paused with one hand on the curtain that blocked off the doorway into the storeroom. Slowly he turned back to her. "No fair," he said in a low voice.

"What?"

"No fair bringing up red long johns." He stepped toward her. By the dim light that crept over the shelving from Charlie's apartment she could barely make out the planes of his face. "You can't evade me one minute and toss out comments like that the next."

"I don't underst—"

"Because what happens is," he barreled on without giving her time to speak, "that my imagination runs wild picturing you in a pair of long underwear, a very snug pair, with every curve outlined, every luscious—"

"I didn't mean to do that," she interrupted, her words whooshing out like air from a balloon.

"Didn't you? I'm not so sure. Is it come hither or stay away? Is it yes or no?"

"You're a fine one to talk. You don't know which you want, either."

"I'm beginning to. How about you?"

"I don't know," she said desperately.

"Just two words, two simple words. One is yes, and the other is no. Which is it?"

"It isn't either," she wailed. "It's . . ."

"Maybe?" He stood inches away and flexed his fingers.

"You're pushing me to say something that I'm not ready to say."

"Then let's not talk about it."

She expected him to turn and push aside the curtain, but instead he reached for her. Before she could react his mouth found hers.

5

"NO," JILL MOANED, but it was too late. Spence's firm lips and coaxing tongue broke through the barrier she'd tried so diligently to erect. Her resistance crumbled. For the moment, choice was gone as she abandoned herself to the surge of emotion that had been gathering strength ever since they met.

His kiss blended the familiar warmth of coming home with the churning excitement of adventure. He promised safety and daring, security and delicious risk. He explored the fit of their bodies with gentle hands that sculpted her curves until she was molded against him like clay, there to discover his growing arousal.

In the space of one kiss, passion had moved from abstract longing to specific need; there was now an empty, aching place within her.

Unaware of the mayhem he was causing, Spence plunged his tongue deeper into her mouth. She forgot her avowed purpose in being here. Nothing mattered but the unspoken language of his lips and tongue and the imprint of his body.

After a timeless moment of give and take, he shuddered and slowly drew back. Sliding both hands up her arms, he rested them on her shoulders and looked into her eyes. His face was in shadow, but she could see his eyes, luminous with feeling. "Time out," he said. His voice was shaky, but she heard his smile in the tone of his voice. "Oh, Jill . . ." He sighed deeply. "Please don't tell me you've kissed anybody else like that recently."

"Not . . . recently." Not ever, she almost said, but shyness prevented total honesty.

"Good." He massaged her shoulders. "I take everything back, by the way."

"Everything?"

"All the speeches about what I don't want happening between us. For me, all bets are off." He drew her close again.

"Spence . . . shouldn't we . . . I'm afraid we're rushing into this."

"Maybe we are." His lips hovered over hers. "At the moment I don't give a damn. All I care about is this." He covered her mouth and built on the foundation of desire he'd laid before.

Her breathing quickened in response. She tightened her grip on his shoulders as she sought balance in the whirlpool of sensation he created. Fiery images of loving him flashed like red neon through her mind. The images stretched far into the future, blotting out everything else in her life. But she couldn't let that happen. She might sample this passion, but she had to control it. Had to. In a minute.

He lifted his mouth to speak her name with tender seductiveness.

"You're very dangerous," she said, breathing hard.

"Dangerous?" He laughed softly.

"All my life I've allowed myself to be distracted, to take another route than the one I've chosen." She paused to catch her breath. "I can't do that with this trip."

"I didn't ask you to."

"You don't have to ask. Just by being who you are, you'll make me forget my deadline, scuttle my plans."

"I can't change who I am," he said quietly.

"Of course not, but I can change my reaction to you."

"You can try."

Gratefully she leaped upon the flash of his ego as a weapon to fight her desire. "So you imagine yourself irresistible?" She stepped out of the circle of his arms.

"I wasn't talking about my appeal," he said evenly. "From the way you kissed me, I figured some powerful emotions were stirred up."

"Maybe so," she acknowledged. "But I told you what was at stake. I told you a man was waiting back home for my answer. How can I allow this to go on? Isn't that unfair to him?"

"You're asking the wrong guy that question."

"Aaron loves me."

"That's his choice, Jill. It doesn't give him any rights unless you return his love. So maybe that's the question. Do you?"

She hesitated. "I . . . thought I did."

"Did you tell him that you loved him?"

Jill shook her head. "No, but he thinks that's because I don't know my own mind about anything."

"And what do you think?" Spence said gently.

Her brain whirled. She couldn't think of anything when he was so close. "Everything used to be so clear. I promised myself that I'd stay away from this sort of thing so I could figure out my feelings about Aaron."

"Maybe without 'this sort of thing' you'll never figure it out," he suggested.

She pressed her fingertips to her throbbing temples. "I don't know. I just don't know."

His tone gentled. "Okay. I asked you to help with the mall protest. Maybe we should concentrate on that and leave this other subject alone for a while," he said, reaching out to stroke her hair.

His touch felt so good. She longed to snuggle against him and forget all about Aaron and her guilt about his devotion to her. "Yes," she said, "maybe we should leave it for now."

"Ready to pick out your merchandise?"

"Sure."

He pulled back the curtain. "After you."

She walked past him, holding her breath, as if just the smell of him might topple her shaky resolve. Once under the stark fluorescent lights, she felt stronger and more able to cope. As she began strolling the aisles looking for what she needed in the way of camping gear, Charlie returned, breathless from his walk.

His eyes were bright as he glanced from Spence to Jill. "Did you two have a nice chat while I was gone?"

Jill couldn't manage to utter a casual reply. A simple yes stuck in her throat and she appealed mutely to Spence to fill the silence.

"We . . . seem to have a lot in common," he said, sending a tiny smile Jill's way.

Charlie gazed at them benevolently. "I rather thought you might," he said.

ALTHOUGH HE WAS halfway expecting her, surprise and fascination jolted Spence to a stop when he walked out of his office Friday afternoon and saw her on the other side of the display windows. Painting was a sensuous activity, he realized, especially when viewed this way, facing the artist.

He watched as her mouth pursed in concentration and he ran his tongue over his upper lip, remembering Wednesday night. Oh, she'd been sweet to kiss, this woman who stood there outlining a sock on the glass with practiced brush strokes. He'd read somewhere that a soft paintbrush was a wonderful love toy. Especially, he thought, in the hand of someone creative like Jill. Her artistic nature and vagabond life-style had hooked him. With a woman like Jill, no telling what he might—

His erotic musings were interrupted when she became aware of him and stopped painting. For a moment she held his gaze and he wondered how many of his thoughts were reflected there for her to see. Was there an answering spark in those green eyes, or was that wishful thinking on his part? She broke contact and dipped her brush in the paint.

"Spencer, my boy, she has the look of a woman contemplating romance," Charlie said from near Spence's elbow.

Spence jumped. "No fair sneaking up on me like that!"

"I most certainly did not sneak," Charlie said with an injured expression. "You were so immersed in contemplating our Jill that an entire regiment of soldiers could have marched up behind you unnoticed."

Spence scratched his ear and glanced away. "That obvious, huh?"

"No matter. She feels the same way about you."

"I hope so, Charlie. But she's all hung up on this Aaron guy back home. Thinks she owes him something because he's crazy about her."

"I saw the expression on her face just now. She can't escape her destiny any more than you can, my boy. Now go on out and talk to her. Break the ice."

"Well, actually, I should make sure she's all set for the meeting tonight."

Charlie nodded. "Excellent. Excellent. Perhaps then you can move from practical matters to more romantic ones."

"And, Charlie, speaking of romance, here comes your lady love."

"Gladys?" Charlie turned. "I didn't think she had an interest in the great outdoors."

"I don't think she's here to shop," Spence said with a chuckle. "Except perhaps for a husband."

"Husband? Good gracious, I'm not husband material, my boy. I'm a transient, a ne'er-do-well, a tramp, if you will."

"Right, Charlie. And I'm Donald Duck," Spence murmured in an undertone. "Well, hello, Gladys," he said brightly as she approached. "Charlie and I were just discussing the merits of camping out."

"I'm dying to try camping," Gladys said, "and I'll do it the minute someone invents an inflatable Hilton."

Charlie looked puzzled. "An inflatable Hilton? Spencer, do we carry that brand?"

She winked at Spence. "Don't you just love him? He never gets any of my jokes, but that makes him all the more adorable."

Charlie opened his mouth to comment, but she rushed on.

"Spence, I have a message from Robert about the meeting tonight. He, Bernie and George want to come. So do I, for that matter."

"I don't see why not," Spence replied. "The meeting's not secret. Charlie's planning to come."

"Wouldn't miss it," Charlie confirmed.

"Robert feels that the Senior Striders need a role in this," Gladys said. "We've been strictly a recreational and social group, but we think some advocacy is in order.

These changes Tippy wants will hit the old and infirm hardest. Most of us are in the first category and eventually we'll fall into the second."

"Nonsense, Gladys," Charlie said gruffly. "You'll always be fit as a fiddle."

She flashed him a wicked smile. "And ready for love, as the rest of that expression goes?"

Spence watched in amazement as Charlie blushed. Apparently Spence wasn't the only one being distracted by a member of the fairer sex. He grinned as Charlie cleared his throat and struggled for a witty response that never came.

"Never mind, Charlie." Gladys patted his arm. "I didn't mean to get you all flustered. What I really came by for was to invite you to skate with me on the pond. You mentioned that you know how, and I think we should take a few turns around the ice, my treat."

"Terrific idea, Charlie," Spence said, having a great time with this budding romance between Charlie and Gladys. "Skating will strengthen your ankles and you may even improve your race-walking that way."

"Is that so?" Charlie straightened his tie and strove for his usual dignity. "I could use some improvement there, certainly." He turned to Gladys. "But it hardly seems appropriate for you to pay for both of us, my dear."

Gladys eyed him fondly. "You simply have to get in step with the times, you sweet man. I have a generous income from my husband's life insurance and you are temporarily low on funds. These days, if a woman is in better financial circumstances than a man, she treats. Simple as that."

"She's right, Charlie," Spence added. "Go on and have fun."

Charlie glanced at him and touched the gold figure-eight pin on his lapel. "I have the strangest feeling you're reversing our roles at this moment, Spencer."

"Anything wrong with that?" Spence said with a smile. "You scratch my back and I'll scratch yours."

"Your back itches? Calamine lotion is—"

Gladys took Charlie's arm and propelled him away. "That's just a figure of speech, Charlie," she explained as she guided him toward the front of the store. Her voice drifted back to Spence as they walked away: "Honestly, you take everything so literally. Spence meant that he'd do you a favor if you'll do one for him. Are you helping Spence in some way?"

Spence couldn't hear Charlie's answer as the couple left the store. Spence wondered if Charlie would tell Gladys about Valentine's Day and fate. Come to think of it, was Charlie subject to the same principles? Still mulling over that idea, Spence walked toward the front of the store and the dark-haired woman who was supposed to be his destiny.

She glanced up when he came through the door. "Does this look okay?" she asked, gesturing toward the window.

"Great." He surveyed the white thermal socks with red elastic hanging by their toes on a string of tiny hearts. She was a whiz with that paintbrush. Then he remembered his paintbrush fantasies and felt warmth rising in his cheeks. He was probably blushing the way Charlie had a moment ago. "What have you planned for the other window?" he asked, not caring a whit, but needing small talk to counteract his tendency to think bawdy thoughts.

"I thought maybe a big red kerosene lantern with the slogan of 'Light up your lover's life.'"

"A lantern sounds perfect," he said, entranced by the translucent skin of her throat. "Still ready for the meeting tonight at seven?"

"Sure." She tucked dark curls behind one ear, revealing a ruby-red earring in the shape of a heart.

"I put Charlie and his Senior Strider buddies to work delivering the flyers," he said, mesmerized by the contrast of the blood-red heart against the white skin of her earlobe. "I've had several calls about the meeting," he blundered on, hoping his conversation made sense. "It seems just about every store in the mall will be represented."

Jill nodded. "Good. Speaking of Charlie, I saw him taking off with his friend . . . is it Gladys?"

"That's right." He decided to use this change of topic to his advantage and work around to more personal subjects. "Gladys would like to be much more than Charlie's friend, unless I'm misreading all the signals she's putting out. Frankly, I think a match between those two would be a great idea. She has the money and Charlie has the charm."

Jill laughed and returned to her painting. "What a riot. First Charlie tries frantically to fix you up with someone and now you're doing the same thing to him. You two deserve each other."

"You don't believe in Charlie's theories about fated lovers?" he asked, keeping his tone light.

"Afraid not." She plied her brush with deft strokes and didn't elaborate.

He watched her impatiently. Charlie had said that she was a woman contemplating romance, and that he could tell from her expression that she wanted Spence as much as he wanted her. Spence wished he could believe that, yet she was acting totally indifferent at the moment.

He, on the other hand, was itching to grab her and kiss the living daylights out of those pursed lips. "You think you have a choice or something? That you can decide 'okay, I'm ready now,' and fall in love?"

Still, she wouldn't look at him. "I think I have the choice *not* to fall in love if the timing is wrong, if that's what you mean."

"No kidding?" He stepped closer, wanting to rattle her, get some response, any response. "That opinion doesn't square with the way you reacted in my arms Wednesday night. You melted against me like soft ice cream." He noted with satisfaction that she'd lifted her brush from the window and her hand was trembling.

"I wasn't thinking straight Wednesday night."

"Or perhaps you're not thinking straight now."

She stuck her brush in a jar of water and put the jar in her paint caddy. "Excuse me, but I have the other window to do," she said, picking up the caddy and moving around him.

"You haven't painted the slogan on this one," he reminded her, delighted that his presence bothered her enough to make her move away. That was a start.

"I'll letter both slogans at once. Now, let's see. The sleeping bags should be red, and—"

"Sleeping bags?" he said, leaning casually against the wooden frame of the window. "I thought you said a lantern on this window?"

She flushed. "You're right, of course. I meant lantern. A red lantern with—"

"I can't forget what your lips felt like—so supple, so giving. You tasted wonderful," he said, watching her pupils grow larger.

"Spence, please . . ."

"I could feel your heartbeat, too, fluttering like a bird against me," he murmured, drawing the noose of emotion tighter.

"Don't," she pleaded, gazing at him with her moist lips parted, her eyes soft. "It's not fair."

"It's not fair that you'd kiss me like that and then want to take back all those feelings we shared," he countered, rejoicing in the passion in her eyes. "Have you been able to bury those feelings, Jill? Because I sure as hell haven't been successful."

She didn't speak, but he got his answer just by looking at her. If the mall hadn't been filled with people, he would have made his point by kissing her again and showing her how close to the surface those emotions raged. For now, the knowledge that she was susceptible to him would carry him through the day.

"See you tonight," he whispered, and pushed himself away from the windowframe. Unable to walk calmly back into the store and return to his bookkeeping chores, he strode down the mall toward the skating pond.

Finding a vacant artificial log, he sat on it and rested his chin in his hands. Across the pond from him, Charlie and Gladys skated as if they'd practiced together for years. Arms around each other's waist, hands linked, they glided with smooth precision, often gazing at each other with fond smiles.

Spence envied them. The course of their relationship ran as smooth as the ice slipping beneath their skates. Neither of them had anyone or anything to consider except themselves. The only obstacle to their happiness was Charlie's reluctance to accept money from Gladys, but Spence figured Charlie would overcome that.

For Spence and Jill, the road was far rougher. His heart was still pounding with suppressed desire and he wrestled with guilt. Who was he to sabotage Jill's determination to finish her trip and return to her lukewarm relationship with Aaron? Yet that was exactly his intent—sabotage. Her journey and whatever it meant to her was standing in his way, and he was used to getting what he went after.

Somehow he had to keep her from leaving until he could show her what lovemaking could be like between them. He wanted to provide her with a powerful reason to dump Aaron and come back to him. Yet he couldn't rush her, either, or the relationship wouldn't stand on solid ground. Would she grant him the time to woo her? After the meeting tonight, after everyone was gone and he could wrap his arms around her again, he'd know the answer.

6

IN THE Remembrance Mall Museum, display cases lined the perimeter of the principal room, and usually an ornate covered buggy sat in the center. When Jill arrived on Friday night she noticed that the buggy had been wheeled to a far corner and folding chairs were arranged in the rows where the buggy had been.

The chairs were already filling with people, some eating carry-out dinners. Jill heard someone joke about tonight's dinner show. Spence stood in the corner next to the buggy with his hand resting affectionately on a large spoked wheel. He was surrounded by Charlie, Gladys and the three men from lunch the other day—Robert, Bernie and George.

Spence hadn't noticed her come in, and she allowed herself a covert assessment before he did. Her feelings for him bubbled to the surface, drawn there by the tilt of his head, the curve of his smile, the strength of his stance. Despite all the warning lights flashing around this attraction, she couldn't put it from her.

To strengthen her resolve she'd called Aaron the night before. She'd wanted him to be warm and flirtatious, to make her decision easier. Instead he'd scolded her about taking on this extra job of the mall protest. "Jill of All Trades is at it again," he'd said, disapproval zinging across the telephone line from Maine. "If you're not going to stick to your plan, you might as well come home now."

They'd fought, something she wasn't used to doing with anyone, least of all Aaron. He'd been so patient with her through all her searching for the right career. Patient and—she realized now—indulgent, as someone might indulge a child's fierce determination to fly airplanes or discover a cure for cancer.

From this distance, halfway across the country from Aaron, Jill understood at last that he didn't care about her struggle over what to do with her life as long as she got it out of her system and settled down with him. He had no particular appreciation for her talents, except when they enlivened his own existence. He viewed her as an adjunct to him, and at the moment, an uncooperative one.

She thought of the way Spence's eyes had lit up when she'd described her cross-country trek. He hadn't warned her about the danger of her plan, or asked why in the world she'd decided to do it. He'd simply accepted her behavior as appropriate to the sort of person he saw before him. Jill liked Spence's image of her. Yet he wasn't reluctant to cross her, either, as evidenced by their clash over whether she'd help with this protest. It seemed they could agree and disagree openly.

Added to that was the most compelling physical attraction she'd ever experienced. And he seemed to sense it. No man had ever talked quite as straightforwardly to her about his needs as Spence had today.

She'd been afraid to go back and look at the job she'd done on the lantern after his unsettling speech, she'd painted on auto-pilot for the rest of the day before stowing her supplies in the van.

From the corner of the room, Spence glanced her way and smiled. Jill returned his smile and acknowledged to herself that the internal bargaining had started. She was familiar with the process. A distraction would come along and eventually she'd give herself permission to be distracted from her goal, always promising herself that she'd get back on track and work twice as hard to complete the original project.

Except she'd always allowed the distraction to take over and the project to be forgotten. Aaron expected that to happen again—he'd said so the night before on the telephone, although he knew nothing about the added distraction of Spence Jegger.

Not this time, she vowed, walking over to Spence and the others gathered around him. She wouldn't give Aaron the satisfaction of seeing her fail, and then there was G.G., who'd displayed such faith in her plan. G.G.'s collection of postcards would not end with Denver.

"Ah, Jill," Charlie said, moving aside to make room for her next to Spence in the circle. "Right on time."

"The lantern looks terrific," Spence said, smiling down at her. "In fact, we sold a lantern today because a woman wanted to give it to her husband for Valentine's Day. She said she'd steal your slogan, if you don't mind."

Rattled by his nearness, Jill couldn't remember what slogan he was talking about. "She's welcome to it," she said, and finally remembered lettering the unoriginal phrase "Light up your lover's life" underneath the lantern. Standing so close to Spence, she caught a whiff of his after-shave and her pulse accelerated. She moved away a few more inches, afraid that touching him would add to the turmoil of her senses.

"Nice to see you again, Jill," Robert said, adjusting his glasses.

Jill acknowledged his greeting. "The Senior Striders must be taking quite an interest in this cause," she said.

Bernie shifted his weight and leaned on his walking stick. "We're just observers, at this point."

"That is, unless the tenants all go against Spence," George added. "In that case, we'll speak up."

"Let's hope they all agree with me," Spence said. "Then we can form a delegation, go straight to Tippy and settle this."

"Let's hope," Jill murmured, realizing that if the campaign went that smoothly, she'd be on the road by Monday at the latest. That wasn't nearly enough time to explore her feelings for Spence, yet she'd have no excuse to stay.

Spence glanced at his watch. "It's seven. Let's get going. Jill, if you'll sit in the front row, I'll introduce you and explain your function before we begin."

"Fine."

"We'll sit with her," Charlie said, appointing himself spokesman for the Senior Strider delegation.

Jill and her followers had no trouble finding seats together. The front row was empty. Jill recognized that as an obvious sign that people weren't sure where their loyalties lay.

She settled into the metal chair with a sigh; it felt good to sit down. Behind her a woman finished the last of a hamburger and Jill's mouth watered. She'd skipped dinner and hadn't realized she was hungry until she caught the aroma from the hamburger. Her encounter with Spence that afternoon had driven all thought of food from her mind for several hours. She settled her legal pad on her knees and leaned back in the chair.

Spence stood alone in front of the group and after everyone had quieted down he thanked them for coming and introduced Jill as his consultant.

A consultant, she thought with a smile. Aaron would laugh at that.

"She's not some sort of protest organizer, is she, Spence?" said a man in the back row. "We don't need someone like that around here."

"Jill's not any kind of agitator," Spence said. "She happened to be painting windows in a shopping center that was having trouble with the management and she observed how they solved their problems."

"I'm not having troubles with the management," the man said. "Anybody who wants to raise my profit margin is okay by me."

"I'd like more profit, too," Spence said easily. "But I wonder what we'll sacrifice in our search for it. I've always been proud of operating in the Remembrance Mall, because we seemed to be more than a collection of shopkeepers. We have the trolley and the handi-cars for people who need a lift to get around. We have the melodrama for live entertainment, which also encourages amateur theater, and we have a museum that links us to our heritage. In the name of profit, Tippy Henderson wants to take those things away."

"Yes, but she has a point," said a woman in a tailored suit. "We pay for those amenities, not the general public. She's trying to pass the cost on to the consumers instead of adding it to our bill."

"And when it is our expense," said a man next to her, "we have to raise our prices accordingly, and then we're not competitive with other stores in the city. The Remembrance Mall is a nice place to shop, but it's also an expensive place to shop. I've heard people say that."

"Yeah," agreed the man in the back row. "How many people come here to hang around and do all their buying somewhere else? If Tippy makes them buy something in order to ride the trolley, that makes sense to me."

"And the museum is very nice," said another woman, "but a large department store would lower the rent across the board for all of us. Who wouldn't appreciate that?"

A murmured chorus of assent greeted her comment, and Jill noted the tone of the discussion on her legal pad. Spence was facing an uphill battle, she thought, and wondered how he'd answer these people.

He gazed out over the crowd and rocked back and forth on the balls of his feet. Jill could tell this resistance bothered him. "But the policies Tippy proposes are shortsighted," he said, his voice louder, more commanding. "People often say that shopping malls all over the country are the same, that you could be dropped into one in Des Moines or Syracuse and never know the difference. The concept of the Remembrance challenges that statement, but take away the museum, the melodrama and the trolley and we'll be like every other mall in the country."

"Hey, I'm not in this business to be famous," said the man in the back row. "I'm here to make money."

Spence's jaw clenched and whispers were exchanged among the Senior Striders. Before Spence could respond to the man in the back row, Robert stood and faced the group. "How about the element of compassion, folks?" he said. "I'm in this mall about every day, and I hear the cash registers ringing. I doubt if any of you are really hurting for business. Perhaps you simply want a bigger slice of the pie, and the disabled and poorer customers will be shoved, literally, into the cold by your greed." Robert resumed his seat.

"Who's he?" asked someone amid an undercurrent of angry grumbles.

"Yeah," piped up another person. "What right's he got to—"

"I can tell this isn't going to be a smooth discussion," Spence said, interrupting. "The man who spoke is a member of the Senior Striders. They asked if they could sit in on this meeting as consumer representatives."

"Look, Spence," said the man in the back row. "No offense, but we know you have a soft spot for the old folks, and you've moved one of them into the back of your store. We don't care about that, and the seniors who race-walk are all fine and good, but are they really paying their share of the upkeep around this mall?"

Jill noticed a white line of tension around Spence's mouth. His anger was building. He opened his mouth to answer the man's comment, but he closed it again when his attention was diverted to a late-comer standing at the museum entrance. "Hello, Ms Henderson," he said carefully, and everyone turned to look. "Would you like to join us?"

Tippy Henderson smiled at them. "Well, isn't this a happy group? Since I have you all in one place, perhaps I'll use this chance to mention that those valentine paintings had better be cleaned off all the windows by noon on February fifteenth. I'm all for individual enterprise, but I've hired a design crew for a mall-wide Easter promotion in conjunction with the opening of our new department store, and I don't want any valentine stuff hanging around."

"Do you have the new store lined up?" asked the man in the back.

"Just about. A representative from Anderson's department store chain is flying in tomorrow, and I came by to take another look at the space we have here. I had no idea a meeting was in progress. Don't let me interrupt a thing." Then she took a seat on the end of the back row.

"We've been discussing the new department store, among other things," Spence said to her. "I called this meeting to determine if there's any support for keeping the museum."

"I see." Tippy glanced around. "Is there? Perhaps we should have a show of hands. Although I'm not bound by a vote like that, I like to keep my tenants happy. This space is far too large and valuable for the purpose, of course, but we have a vacancy on the first floor."

"That space is no bigger than a closet," Spence said, his eyes dark and foreboding. "We've aired a few thoughts tonight, and now it's time for some considered judgment on everyone's part. Unless there are objections, I'd like to adjourn the meeting."

"Without a vote?" Tippy said.

"That's right."

"I move we adjourn," said a colorfully dressed woman who hadn't spoken before.

"I second it," said a man beside her.

Spence glanced in their direction. "All in favor, say aye."

Jill expected the chorus of affirmative votes that followed. Tippy's presence had ended any real hope for honest discussion. As everyone stood to file out, the woman who had motioned to adjourn the meeting walked quietly up to Spence. Jill strained to hear what she said but couldn't make it out in the shuffle of feet.

"What a disaster," Charlie said, gazing around at Jill and his Senior Strider friends. "We'd better go up there and give Spencer some moral support."

"I'm appalled at the attitude of these merchants," Bernie commented, tapping his walking stick on the tile floor. "You'd think we were asking them to give their wares away." He glanced at Charlie. "Are you sure it isn't time for me to—"

"Gracious, no," Charlie said quickly. "Not yet."

"Not time for Bernie to do what?" Gladys asked.

"Why, ah . . ." Charlie avoided her gaze. "You know Bernie's a charmer, my dear. I fancy he thinks he could change Ms Henderson's mind about all this."

Bernie flushed but didn't contradict Charlie.

"Why, Bernie, you sly dog!" Gladys teased and Bernie turned a deeper crimson.

"It's a thought," Jill said with a grin. "We should keep it in mind. Anyway, in the meantime we need to instill a sense of unity among the tenants. Right now, everyone's thinking of individual gain."

"That is the problem, of course, my dear!" Charlie beamed at her. "I knew you wouldn't let us down. We must return to Spencer's shop and have a—let me see, I learned a new term from a teenage boy yesterday—a rap session," he finished triumphantly. "That's what we must have."

"Exactly," Jill agreed as they all headed toward Spence.

The first woman had left, but Jill and the rest of the group paused as Tippy Henderson walked briskly forward and stood with arms crossed in front of Spence.

"Decided to make an end run around me, did you?" she said, lifting penciled brows.

The muscles twitched in Spence's jaw. "I tried to talk to you about this. We couldn't come to terms."

"So you're hoping to rally the tenants, I suppose."

"Something like that."

"You won't have time. I'll close the Anderson deal by next week. Besides that, you're wrong, Spence. This is a shopping mall, not some altruistic dream city of the future. We operate to make a profit, not to run a free amusement park. When my corporation bought this mall I asked for the assignment because I knew I could cut flab and boost revenue quickly."

"And ruin a unique concept in the process."

"Ruin? Don't be silly. We'll still have the Victorian gingerbread, the light posts, probably even the trolley, although not quite so loaded down. Have you any idea how much electricity it takes to cart those deadbeats up and down the mall? We'll save on that, too."

Lips pressed in a straight line, Spence started to turn away when she caught his arm. "What's this about some old guy living in the back of your store?"

Jill held her breath. She'd been afraid Tippy had heard that remark.

Spence's eyes narrowed. "It's my store," he said in a low voice.

"And ultimately my corporation's liability. Your family may have owned this property once, but they sold it, Spence. You're not the kingpin around here anymore, and I want that man out of your store. Tonight."

"I don't think so."

"Really? Then you'd better read the fine print on your contract and notify your lawyer, because I intend to press the matter."

"You bi—"

"Spencer, my boy," Charlie said, rushing forward and grabbing him by the arm. "We simply must talk with you. Have you a minute now? Excuse me, madam. Is it Ms Henderson? I'm pleased to make your acquaintance, but we must take this dear boy away from you for a minute."

Jill was amazed at the strength Charlie exhibited as he steered Spence away from Tippy. Robert and George quickly got into the act, and before long they were all barreling down the upper deck of the mall as if they were race-walking.

"I don't care what she threatens, Charlie, you're staying," Spence announced as they all headed for the brass-railed stairway.

"I wouldn't dream of it," Charlie replied, puffing slightly from the pace. "You have enough problems without adding me to the list."

"She could win this one, Spence," Bernie advised, using his walking stick to propel his lanky frame along in step with the others. "Everyone's been willing to look the other way because we all like Charlie, but I wager Tippy can get him evicted."

"I wish my parents had never sold the property," Spence muttered as the contingent hurried into his store.

"How'd it go?" asked Stephanie from behind the cash register.

"Don't ask," cautioned Gladys. "We'll be in conference."

They all crowded into Spence's office. Gladys and Jill took the chairs across from the oak desk and Spence waved Charlie into the swivel desk chair. Robert, Bernie and George leaned against the wall while Spence paced the remaining floor space. For a while no one spoke.

Finally Spence broke the silence. "Maybe if I hired Charlie as my personal night watchman . . ."

"I think you'd have to prove that he's trained in that function," Robert said. "He might even have to carry a gun."

Charlie recoiled in horror. "Never!"

"Well, then I'll think of something else," Spence vowed.

"No, you won't, my boy," Charlie said, leaning his elbows on the desk. "I'm leaving tonight."

"I won't have it," Spence said. "There's snow out there, Charlie, and the temperature will be down in the twenties tonight. No way are you leaving."

"Of course he's leaving," Gladys said. "He'll stay with me." All eyes focused on her.

"Well, if it comes to that, he could stay at my house," Spence said. "I don't know why that didn't occur to me in the first place."

"Or mine," added Bernie.

"I don't have an extra bedroom, but there's the fold-out sofa in the living room," George said. "You're welcome to it, Charlie."

"Same here," said Robert. "The wife and I deliberately cut down on space when we bought the town house, but temporarily we could—"

"This is silly," Gladys said, before Robert could finish. "Improper as you all might consider my suggestion, it makes perfect sense. I have a two-bedroom condo within walking distance of the mall. Why would you want to drag Charlie halfway across town, where the rest of you live, when he can stay with me?"

Jill glanced at Charlie, whose lined face grew redder by the moment. He fiddled with his gold lapel pin and seemed greatly interested in the papers on Spence's desk.

Spence paused in his pacing and looked from Charlie to Gladys. "You may have a point," he said with an almost imperceptible smile. "What do you say, Charlie?"

"I hesitate to inconvenience this dear lady," Charlie said, still looking down at the materials on the desk.

"Nonsense." Gladys scoffed. "You're blind as a bat if you think I'd be inconvenienced."

Charlie coughed and looked up. "Well, then, I, um, accept your generous offer."

"Wonderful."

Jill peeked over at Spence, and they exchanged a smile. She could see now why Charlie enjoyed this matchmaking business. Watching the relationship between Charlie and Gladys unfold gave Jill a real high.

"If that's settled, I suppose we'd better face our second problem." Spence began to pace again. "Tippy's made more headway than I had expected, although we're not entirely without allies. The woman who seconded my motion to adjourn, Hedda Kramer from the candle shop, is behind us, and she says there are others."

"They certainly didn't make themselves known," Bernie grumbled. "All we heard were the money-grubbers."

"Hedda estimates we might have about thirty percent of the tenants in our corner," Spencer said. "It's not a majority, but it's a start."

Jill decided to plunge in. "Thirty percent isn't bad," she said, "and I have an idea for bringing the others into our camp."

"So speak up, my dear," Charlie encouraged.

"The thing is, it will mean an outlay of money."

"Don't worry about that," Spence said. "What's your idea?"

"The tenants' association isn't a cohesive unit," she explained, and then turned in her chair to focus on everyone in the room. "The first step in getting them to pull together for the common good, I think, is to create a team spirit. And they have to believe in the cause."

"Which maybe seventy percent don't," Robert commented.

"I'll bet most of that seventy percent are transplants from other parts of the country," Jill said. "They haven't been given much chance to develop a sense of community, of pride in the history of the region. I think we should take them all on a bus trip, a historical tour of the area. If you throw in some sort of hot dog roast, if the weather's not horrendous, they'll also have a chance to socialize and nurture that feeling of comradery."

Spence's dark eyes glowed with pride. "Great idea."

"I agree," said Robert, and he collected nods of assent from Bernie and George. "If you need funding for this project, let me know, Spence."

Jill gazed at the three men. "I know you're all retired now, but who are you, really?"

"Doesn't matter," Bernie said, leaning on his walking stick and smiling mysteriously. "We're just three old geezers who want to help, that's all."

Jill accepted his nonanswer, but she didn't have to use much imagination to put Bernie in a three-piece suit at the head of a long table in a corporate boardroom.

"The only trouble with the bus trip is that we have to move fast," Spence commented. "Tippy has the Anderson representative coming in tomorrow, and she's bragged about closing the deal by next week."

"I'll start calling the tour bus companies first thing in the morning," Jill said. "I'll set it up as soon as they can do it. Will we have any trouble getting people to come, do you think?"

"I doubt it," Robert said. "We're giving an afternoon's outing for nothing. Who wouldn't welcome a break from routine to ride in a comfortable bus, see the sights and get fed? Incidentally, I know some people who do wonderful catered events, even outdoors, even in the winter. Let me know the day, and I'll arrange the meal."

"That would be expensive," Jill warned.

"Never mind that," Robert said, with an assurance that fed Jill's belief that he, as well as Bernie, had left a lucrative position that provided him with retirement benefits most people only dreamed of.

Spence glanced around at the group assembled in his office. "I'm impressed with the way you've all turned this thing around. We've solved the problem with Charlie and have a good start on the mall situation."

"I think we have to hand it to the women," George said with a chuckle. "They're the ones with the solutions. All we have to do is help implement them."

"You've got that right," Spence agreed with a grin. "Shall we wrap this up? I'm sure you all have other things to do besides deal with this craziness."

"I should get home to the wife," Robert said. "She accuses me of being busier since I retired."

"I have a few projects going, too," Bernie said.

"Yeah, so do I," George added. "Guess we'll leave you folks."

"And Charlie needs to pack," Gladys said when the three men had left.

Charlie stood and walked around the desk. "That won't take long, dear lady. I should warn you that I have very few material possessions in this world. By the way, do you play chess?"

"No, I never learned."

Charlie paused, and Jill worried that this would be a stumbling block for the otherwise compatible couple. Chess obviously meant a great deal to Charlie, considering that his set was apparently the only thing of value he owned, besides his gold lapel pin.

Charlie smiled at Gladys. "Then I shall teach you," he said, and Jill gave a small sigh of relief.

Charlie's leave-taking seemed to go on for a long time. Jill sensed that despite their original bravery, Gladys and Charlie were ambivalent about this major step in their courtship. She understood the feeling. Once Charlie moved into Gladys's condo, there would be no going back to a more casual friendship. She faced a similar crossroads with Spence.

THE MALL WAS CLOSING by the time Gladys and Charlie waved their final farewell and walked together toward the nearest exit. Charlie carried his briefcase and a quilted jacket Spence had forced on him. Jill and Spence watched them until they reached the double glass doors leading outside. They stopped while Charlie put on his new quilted jacket after helping Gladys into her fur-lined suede coat. Then Charlie held the door for Gladys, and they disappeared into the night.

"I hope it works out," Jill said, gazing after them.

"Me, too." Spence guided her back inside and reached for the handle on the metal grid. "I never thought I'd be glad for anything Tippy did, but she may have inadvertently done Charlie a favor." He pulled the heavy door halfway down, then turned to the young woman at the counter. "We'll be in back, Stephanie, if you need anything."

Jill followed him to Charlie's vacated living quarters. "I think your habit of leaving your employees alone to close up is wonderful," she said, standing in the center of the small room. The furnishings were unchanged, except for the absence of the books and the chess set. "That really builds an atmosphere of trust."

"I hope so." Spence waved her to the armchair and she sat down. "I started doing it when Charlie arrived, because the nightly chess games made the whole thing seem natural. Looks like I'll have to get another chess partner." He sat on the edge of Charlie's bed. "Do you play?"

Jill smiled. "Not very well."

"Then maybe I should take a page out of Charlie's book and teach you."

"That doesn't make much sense, considering how soon I'll be leaving."

His expression darkened. "I don't like to think about that. I—"

Stephanie called from the curtained doorway. "Spence? I've totaled out the cash drawer."

"Be right there," he called back. "Don't go away," he said to Jill, as he got to his feet. "I'll let her out the front and lock up."

"I should probably leave with her," Jill said, starting to rise from the chair.

He paused. "I wish you wouldn't."

She met his gaze and her skin tingled. Charlie was gone. In a few minutes, Stephanie would be gone, too. Neither Jill nor Spence could pretend that there was more business to transact. All that could be said about the mall project had been said in Spence's office. If Jill agreed to stay, it could only be for one reason. Heart pounding, she looked into his eyes.

7

JILL SWALLOWED; her throat was dry. "All right," she said.
"Thank you."

Spence's quiet gratitude shook her. He wore no smile
of triumph, just a look of appreciation. Perhaps she
wasn't being so foolish, after all.

"I'll be right back," he murmured.

When he left, Jill leaned against the chair and took a
deep breath. It didn't help; her heartbeat still seemed
unnaturally fast and her hands were clammy. She'd
agreed to stay, but now she wasn't sure what that im-
plied, exactly. Perhaps she'd better decide before he returned, she thought.

Her gaze drifted to the single bed and she trembled. He
couldn't expect . . . No matter, she wouldn't allow matters to progress to that stage. She merely wanted to explore the feelings between them, to find out if the magic
of his kiss still affected her the way she remembered from
two nights ago.

But they would be alone, with no Charlie to interrupt
them. One kiss would lead to another, and another . . .
Nervousness drove her from the chair and sent her
prowling around the small cubicle. How typical of her,
she thought, to say yes to something without fully exploring the consequences.

She heard the metal door clang shut on the entrance
to the store and knew that Stephanie was gone. She considered making the excuse that she'd skipped dinner, but

he'd probably offer to buy her something, and she definitely wasn't hungry anymore. What could she possibly say to him that wouldn't sound foolish, as if she didn't know her own mind? Jill of All Trades was vacillating again.

Feeling trapped by her impulsiveness, she kept moving around the small room while waiting for him to reappear. Eventually she heard his footsteps on the cement of the storeroom floor. She faced the makeshift doorway.

He walked through the opening and stopped, his smile of anticipation fading. "You look like a caged animal."

"I . . ." She turned away, embarrassed.

"What is it?"

"I don't know you. You don't know me. You probably think . . ." She couldn't finish.

"I probably think what?" He crossed the room and stood near her, waiting.

She steeled herself. Something had to be said. "I won't go to bed with you tonight."

His concern mellowed into gentleness. "Okay," he said with a slow smile.

"I mean it." She cringed at her defensive tone. It sounded as if she were trying to convince herself as well as him.

"Good. Then we're in agreement on that subject."

She blinked. "We are?"

"Sure." He reached for her as though he was approaching a skittish animal. "Hey, Jill," he said softly, drawing her closer, "I know our time together is limited, but that's no excuse to rush and bungle everything. I plan to give this as much time as it deserves."

"I was afraid. . . I mean, there is a bed in here." She felt the warmth of his body through the soft cotton of his blue turtleneck, and her arms seemed to slip automatically over his shoulders.

"And maybe we'll lie on it together." He pressed his lips to her forehead.

"I don't think that's a good—"

"You gave me your trust when you agreed to stay for a while." He kissed her temple. "I won't violate your trust, Jill."

"Perhaps you wouldn't mean to, but we're very much alone, and it would be easy to get carried away." So easy, she thought, as his slow kisses over her face replaced her tension with a languid willingness to be loved.

"Yes, we're very much alone." He traced the curve of her cheek with his lips. "But I didn't plan it, didn't plan for it." He leaned back and smiled at her. "Even if I had all sorts of seduction techniques in mind, I couldn't follow through. The Drug Mart is closed."

"What?"

"You know. The drugstore, where they sell—"

"Oh." She flushed. "Well, of course I didn't even think about that."

He traced the line of her chin with one finger. "Maybe you imagine I keep something on hand at all times?"

"Not necessarily. For all I know you think that I—"

He shook his head. "Nope. Not in keeping with what you've told me about this trip."

"I like the fact that you're unprepared, too," she admitted, stroking the back of his neck. "Once you knew Charlie would be at Gladys's house tonight, you could have made some excuse and dashed off to the drugstore."

"Honesty time. I thought of it."

"But you didn't do it," she said softly. She was melting for this man. He was more than she'd dared hope.

"No. I wanted to put the brakes on myself. I—" He paused and glanced away. "This sounds corny."

"Try me."

He gazed at her. "I'm beginning to believe Charlie's right. When I look at you, I see... You'll think I'm crazy."

What she thought was that he was wonderful. Spence had announced that he wouldn't make love to her tonight. He had no ulterior motive for telling her how he felt, yet he was struggling to put tender emotions, emotions men seldom expressed, into words. "I'm listening," she murmured, gazing into his eyes. "Tell me."

"I see the future, Jill," he said. "I have the uncanny feeling I'll be looking into those green eyes of yours twenty, thirty, forty years from now. I've been married before, and I never had that feeling, even then."

A shiver ran down her spine. "Are you sure it's not the persuasiveness of a very dear old man that has you thinking this way?"

"I tell myself that all the time." His dark gaze searched hers. "And then I look into your eyes."

"I know what you're talking about." She ran her tongue over her lips. "I have no business being here tonight, but I . . . couldn't leave."

He nodded. "I saw the struggle on your face, and I saw you give in to it. When you did, something clicked into place for me. Oh, Jill," he murmured, pulling her close and cradling her head against his chest. "You're like a gift." He chuckled softly. "A gift I'm determined to take my time opening. But when you're in my arms, and I can smell your perfume and touch your hair—" he leaned down and combed her hair behind her ear "—and kiss all the soft places waiting for me . . ."

Jill sighed as his breath tickled her earlobe.

"This little heart drove me wild this afternoon." He outlined the earring with his tongue. "A flash of red against that white skin . . . I wanted to grab you, in front of everyone, and . . . mmm, that's it, relax a little . . . Just . . . relax . . ."

Jill's eyes drifted shut as his lips caressed her throat, her chin, her cheeks. Vaguely she realized that despite all he'd said, Spence was a practiced lover and she had better remain on her guard. But this seemed so innocent, this trail of kisses that soothed her like slow music. His hands stayed in one place, pressed against the small of her back while his mouth played over her face and throat.

Muscles tight from the long day eased and her head fell back. "This is better than meditation," she murmured.

"I should hope so." Kissing the corners of her mouth, he began a slow massage along her spine.

"Ever had chiropractic training?" she mumbled as his gentle kneading gradually transformed her into a rag doll.

"Never." He nuzzled the hollow of her throat.

"You'd be very good at it. You'd—" She stopped talking as he kissed his way down to the first button of her blouse. Somewhere amid all the relaxation he'd cultivated, a seed of desire was growing, and Jill knew that innocence had ended when his lips reached the barrier of her clothing. And she wanted him to go on.

He stopped kissing her; his hands were still. She opened her eyes and met his intense gaze. Then slowly he reached for her wrist and unfastened the button at her cuff.

"You won't forget what you said?" she whispered, her heart thundering as he moved to the other sleeve.

"I won't forget." He held her gaze and paused at the top button at the front of her blouse. "Can you trust me not to?"

"I have . . . no choice," she breathed, breathless with the need to be touched.

Fire burned in his eyes. He nudged the button from its mooring and stroked the valley between her breasts with the back of his hand. She gripped his shoulders, her legs growing weak.

One by one the buttons surrendered to his steady advance until at last he drew out the hem of her blouse and finished the job. Taking her hands from his shoulders, he slid the garment down over her arms and tossed it on the chair. Without looking away, he unhooked her bra and threw it on top of her blouse. Only then did he shift his gaze to her unfettered breasts. A shudder eddied through him.

Her nipples tightened under his attention and a sweet throbbing began deep within her.

"Lie with me," he whispered.

She couldn't have remained standing had he asked her to. Weak with desire, she nodded.

He led her to the iron cot and kicked off his still-laced running shoes.

She followed suit before stretching out on the worn blanket. "Take off your shirt," she whispered.

He tugged the hem of his turtleneck free and crossed his arms to pull it over his head. She watched, relishing the way he sucked in his flat belly as he whipped the shirt over his head. She'd imagined his muscled beauty from the outline beneath his shirt, from the feel of his body against hers. Now she held out her arms to the reality with a thrill of anticipation.

The springs of the old bedstead squeaked under his weight as he lay down and gathered her to him. He sighed deeply when she pressed her aching breasts against his chest, rubbing back and forth, tantalizing him with gentle friction.

"So soft," he murmured against the curve of her neck. "So soft, except here . . ." He moved away a fraction and stroked her nipple with his thumb.

Sensation rippled through her, and he stroked her again, absorbing her shiver of delight. And again, as his mouth found hers and he delved knowingly inside. She arched her back, thrusting her breast into the waiting palm of his hand and moaned as he gently squeezed her heated flesh.

Rolling over her, he levered himself on one elbow and caressed her while exploring her mouth with a thoroughness that left her gasping. Yet she knew this was only the beginning. He gazed down at her, then braced his arms on either side of her and kissed her chin, her throat, her collarbone . . .

A wanton madness took hold of her, and she cupped her breasts and offered herself to him.

"Oh, Jill," he breathed, and eagerly took the nipple she lifted toward his mouth.

The moist suction swirled from her breast through her body and she moved restlessly, sensuously. He moved his hips against hers, but layers of denim denied them the contact they craved. Still nuzzling her breasts, he moved to one side and fumbled with the snap of her jeans.

"Spence," she gasped, afraid his control had dissolved; hers was certainly disappearing fast. This passion had ignited far more quickly than either of them could have anticipated.

"It's okay," he breathed against her skin. "It's okay." He opened the zipper, and slipped his hand beneath the elastic of her panties.

The shock of his touch, right where she needed so desperately to be touched, made her groan and close her thighs against his assault. She was drenched with desire, and if she allowed him to touch her again, he'd soon know how quickly he'd aroused her to a fever pitch.

"Don't close me out," he murmured.

She turned her face away. "You must think I'm shameless to want you so much, so soon."

"Shameless?" His voice was thick with passion. "I hope so. Shame has no place here with us."

"I thought we could . . . just hold each other. I didn't mean for this—"

"Hush," he crooned, burrowing his fingers through the triangle of damp hair. "Let me make you happy."

Her thighs began to tremble as he coaxed them apart. She looked at him through dazed eyes. "Men don't act like this."

He smiled. "They don't? Then maybe you haven't met the right man."

"What—what about you?"

"Don't worry about me." He began a slow, sensuous rhythm with his fingers. "Tell me how this feels."

"You know. You must know."

"How could I? I'm a man. Tell me."

"An ache," she said, breathing hard, "but a good ache. Heat. Winding up tight, like the . . . spring . . . on a watch."

"You're beautiful," he said, brushing her mouth with his. "Your eyes are so bright."

"Spence . . ." She arched upward as he penetrated deeper.

"Let go, Jill." He caressed her with firm strokes. "Let it happen."

"I can't—I—oh!" Ecstasy seized her and her cries of wonder were muffled against his mouth as he covered her lips with his own, drinking in her passion.

As her cries subsided, his kisses became feather-soft and he accompanied them with whispered endearments. Gently he refastened her jeans. Stroking her back, he cradled her on the narrow bed.

She wrapped her arms around him and pressed her lips to the mat of hair on his chest. "This seems unfair," she murmured.

"No," he said softly. "I loved doing that for you."

"But you must be suffering . . ."

"I can take it," he said, combing his fingers through her tumbled hair. "Maybe I even wanted to prove that I could, to you and to me. I've been thinking a lot lately about why things didn't work out in my marriage. I've decided a lot of it had to do with selfishness, on both our parts."

"What just happened was certainly unselfish of you," Jill said, looking up into his face.

"Maybe." He smiled at her. "The funny thing is, I enjoyed every minute, although there was a little, uh, added pressure to deal with. But I think that was good for me, for a change."

"Have you had so many lovers?"

"No," he said gently. "No. But when I've wanted someone, I've been an impatient man who demanded compliance from her, immediate gratification for me. It occurred to me that there was a better approach. At least, I hope it was better."

She traced the laugh lines around his mouth. "I don't think you have to wonder."

"Feed my ego. Tell me anyway."

"I've never felt more vulnerable in my life . . . or more cherished."

He gazed at her with satisfaction. "I like that. And you were."

"Which? Vulnerable or cherished?"

"Cherished." He cupped her chin in one hand. "Definitely cherished."

She absorbed his delight at having pleased her. Deep within her echoed the memory of tension that he'd released so gloriously, tension that he must still feel. She eased away from him and slowly located the fastening at the waistband of his jeans.

"No." He covered her hand.

"Don't argue," she whispered, pressing downward, encountering his fullness.

"I didn't expect . . ." His voice faltered as she rubbed her hand over the taut denim.

"I know." She reached for the fastening again and this time he didn't stop her. The zipper parted easily, assisted by his thrusting manhood.

He gasped as she drew the elastic of his briefs down and wrapped her fingers around him. "Now who's vulnerable?" he asked, breathing hard.

"Cherished," she murmured, sliding her hand down the smooth shaft. She trembled with excitement at the prospect of experiencing his passion this way first. He must have felt the same sense of daring discovery with her, she thought, caressing the silken length of him. She pressed a sensitive spot with her thumb and he moaned. "Good?" she asked, watching his face.

"You know it." His eyes closed as she stroked more firmly. "Jill . . . yes . . . that's so . . ."

"I'm glad," she said, understanding his unspoken words of praise. She could tell his control was slipping, and she touched him more boldly, seeking his final surrender. He moaned again when she increased the pressure and pace of her seductive rhythm. At last he tensed, then cried out as his warmth cascaded over her hand.

Long moments later he slowly opened his eyes and sighed happily. "So much for altruism."

"It seemed only fair."

"Lady, that was several grades higher than fair."

"Good."

"A few moments ago I had myself talked into letting you go back to your campground tonight. Now I'm debating whether to ask you to come home with me."

"Is that what you want?"

"Yes. But no." He pulled a handkerchief from his back pocket and gently wiped her hand. "We'll put our clothes back on, and I'll walk you to your van. I've got to learn patience. One of the reasons I'm at odds with Tippy Henderson is that I allowed myself to blow up at her instead of quietly trying to change her mind." He adjusted his clothing and climbed from the small bed.

"Is that what you're trying to do with me? Quietly change my mind?"

He helped her to her feet. "If you're talking about your friend Aaron, yes."

"I . . . I've thought about Aaron a lot recently."

"That's discouraging," he said, fastening her bra and kissing her bare shoulder. "I'd rather you thought about me."

"I've thought about you, too."

"I'm glad." He slipped her blouse over her arms and pulled it closed across her breasts.

"I don't love Aaron," she said, looking deep into his eyes.

"I could have told you that."

"Why didn't you?"

He grinned. "I had more fun proving it."

"Mmm." She smiled at him. "But loving him or not loving him doesn't change what I have to do. I intend to be back in Maine before my birthday, as planned. There's still G.G., and more important, there's me. Finishing this trip on time has become tied to my self-respect. Can you understand that?"

"I can try."

"No matter how much I want to, I can't stay here any longer than we've agreed. I can't risk jeopardizing my schedule."

He sipped lingeringly at her lips while he refastened her buttons. "In that case," he murmured, "I'll have to give you plenty of reason to come back."

She didn't doubt that he could. His lazy kisses were making her regret their mutual decision to end the evening.

He finished buttoning her blouse and backed away. "Now we'd better get your coat on, and the rest of my clothes, before all this virtuous self-restraint flies out the window." He put on his shirt and picked up her coat from the chair. "Here you go. I'll walk you out to your van."

His pronouncement struck a sour note with her; it was something Aaron might have announced he'd do, to protect her. "That's really not necessary. I've been walking myself out every night so far. And I'm not naive. I carry mace in my shoulder bag."

He smiled and took his own jacket from a hook on the wall. "I'm not doing this for you. Undoubtedly, after seven months on the road, you're perfectly capable of taking care of yourself. It's one of the things I admire about you. But I want to see where you live so I can picture you dreaming away inside your van tonight."

"It's kind of an old van."

"Then I'll bet you make small repairs on it yourself, too."

"A few," she admitted.

"Come on Wonder Woman," he said, chuckling as he took her arm and guided her toward the back exit of the store. "You're beginning to make me feel inadequate, with all these talents of yours."

As they stepped into the cold, dry air of a Colorado winter night, Jill had a startling insight—Aaron was intimidated by her various abilities, and that was why he teased her about being mistress of none of them. She'd always envied Aaron because he'd decided on his career early. She supposed he was a good dentist, although when he worked on her he was rough, but Aaron knew precious little about anything besides teeth and gums.

"I don't believe Aaron loves me any more than I love him," she said, her breath fogging the air in front of them.

"Probably not," Spence said, tucking her hand into his coat pocket. "But where did that come from, all of a sudden?"

"Oh, I was just thinking." She walked with him over the frost-encrusted asphalt to the pool of lamplight where her van sat in the nearly deserted parking lot. One of the other three cars in the lot had to be Spence's, she thought, and guessed it might be the black Trans Am. "Did you mean what you said about feeling inadequate around me?"

"Well, men are conditioned to imagine they're superior to women in some areas." He glanced at her and grinned. "Like plumbing, for instance."

"But you really don't feel inadequate, do you?"

"Fortunately, no. I was teasing you back there. Shoot, with your ideas, we'll stymie Tippy the Lip in no time. I consider myself lucky to know a woman like you." He laughed. "One who could fix my sink, work on my car and paint me a picture to hang over the fireplace, all in the same afternoon, probably."

Jill laughed, too. "Not quite."

"Seriously though, I do." He released her hand and put his arm around her shoulders as they neared the van. "I do consider myself lucky."

"That's good. That's very good."

He squeezed her shoulder. "Do you have this Aaron business figured out, then?"

"I think so."

"That's a relief. After the way you kissed me that first night, I couldn't imagine there was much between you. But still, I have a conscience and the guy's not here to protect his interests."

"I know now that he never had any interests to protect. It's hard to believe that a week ago I thought I might marry him someday. That seems incredible to me, after..." She hesitated. The wonderful moments they'd shared seemed too intimate to discuss out here in the impersonal emptiness of the parking lot.

His grip tightened around her shoulders. "Nothing's been the same for me since the first night I held you." They reached the van and he brought her around to face him. "You've been in my thoughts nearly every waking minute, and lots of the sleeping ones, too. Charlie thinks there's something magic about Valentine's Day, but the magic's already happened for me. You're incredible, Jill."

"You too," she murmured, wanting to kiss and be kissed, and to forget all this nonsense about going slow and sleeping alone tonight.

He closed his eyes. "Oh, Jill, if you only knew what that liquid look of yours does to me."

Her heart pounded. "Are we being silly to wait?"

"No." He opened his eyes. "But I have to get you into this rolling apartment and on your way before I crawl in after you, drugstore or no drugstore."

"There are twenty-four-hour drugstores," she said, hardly believing her own boldness.

"Don't mention them. I'm a weak man." He steered her around to the driver's side of the van. "I sure wish you weren't leaving town so soon, though. I'm trying to understand this deadline you've imposed on yourself, but—" He stopped and stared at the van for several seconds. "Okay," he said with a lopsided smile. "I know when I'm beat."

"You like my map?"

"I do." He cocked his head to one side and studied the outline of forty-eight states that she'd obviously painted with painstaking care. Thirty-three states were filled in with rainbow colors, and the state capital of each marked and labeled in gold. Beneath the map, also lettered in gold, was the message "Through the Great Forty-Eight," and the dates of her last birthday and her next, when the trip was scheduled to end.

"When do you paint each one?" he asked. "Colorado's still blank."

"When I cross the state line into the next state. I make a little ceremony out of it. People at the roadside rest stops get a real kick out of my insanity."

He gazed down at her. "You're not insane. You're whimsical and creative, and I'd be a fool to tamper with a spirit like yours and try to mold you to my way. I'll have to be grateful for what time you give me, Jill Amory."

"You have me for a few more days," she said, her heart full with his understanding.

"A few more days." He sighed. "Okay. First on the agenda, I'd like you to come to dinner at my parents' house tomorrow night. I've mentioned how you're helping with the mall situation, and they'd love to meet you."

"That sounds nice. I accept."

"And then . . ." His gaze wrapped her in soft velvet. "After dinner, and a decent interval of afterdinner conversation, I want you to come home with me."

She couldn't speak as the passion in his eyes fueled her own.

"Will you?"

"Yes," she whispered.

8

THE NEXT MORNING Jill sat at Spence's oak desk drinking coffee and forced herself to think about tourist bus lines. He'd left her alone to make the calls while he worked with Stephanie and Horace, taking inventory. She couldn't have concentrated at all had he stayed in the office with her. His mere presence in the store, the sound of his voice or his laughter, made thinking difficult. She wondered how he was carrying on so easily with the day's work, given what they had planned for tonight.

At lunchtime Charlie brought her a corndog and some lemonade.

"Spence told me to take care of you," he said, opening his own bag. "You seemed to enjoy our lunch together before, so . . ."

"This is great, Charlie." She couldn't bear to tell him that she wasn't as big a corndog fan as he, or that food was the least of her concerns today.

"Any success with the tour buses?"

"It looks as if we'll have to take two not-very-new buses or none at all, if we want to schedule the tour this week," she replied. "I have to check with Spence and find out whether he wants to take a chance on older buses. All the others are booked."

"I daresay he'll tell you to take a chance," Charlie said, dipping his corndog in a small container of mustard. "He's worried that Tippy will have the department store signed up very soon and the museum shipped down to the vacant space where the shoe outlet used to be."

"We need to keep that from happening," Jill agreed. "I thought we'd draw up a petition demanding that the museum be kept where it is, and after the bus tour we can ask everyone to sign it."

"Splendid idea," Charlie said. He finished his corndog and wiped his hands on a paper napkin. "Well, I mustn't keep you too long." He stuffed the napkin and the empty lemonade cup in his paper bag.

"You don't have to rush off, Charlie." Jill discovered the old man's chatter was a welcome distraction from her heady thoughts about Spence. "Tell me how you're getting along with Gladys."

"Oh!" Charlie flushed. "Why, ah, we're doing just fine, my dear." He shifted in his chair. "Matter of fact, I'm meeting Gladys in a short while for another turn around the ice on the skating pond."

"Is that right?" Jill smiled. "That's why you're anxious to be out of here. You have a date."

"Well, I wouldn't exactly call it a date."

"Why not?"

"We are just good friends, Gladys and I," he said, rolling the top of his sack down then rolling it back up again.

"I hope you are good friends. That makes everything so much nicer. But, Charlie, Gladys looks at you the way a chocolate freak looks at a hot fudge sundae. And I've caught you looking back. So don't try to pull this 'only friends' business around me."

To Jill's surprise, Charlie's discomfort increased. "Alas, but you're right," he said, sounding distressed. "I find Gladys extremely attractive."

"What's so terrible about that? She's even rich, besides."

"Yes," Charlie wailed. "She's everything I could want. Fate is so unkind."

"Unkind? Charlie, I don't get it. You should be over-joyed, not moaning pitifully about the situation." She narrowed her eyes at him. "Surely you're not allowing pride to stand in the way of happiness for both of you?"

Charlie shook his head. "Not pride, my dear. I'm just not . . . able . . . to indulge in such matters."

She was stunned into silence. Apparently the poor man was struggling with impotence. He probably hadn't been with a woman in years, and now the pressure to perform was too much. Jill's heart went out to him. "Maybe you haven't given this enough time," she said gently. "After all, you only moved into Gladys's house last night."

"I'm afraid time will only make everything more dif-ficult," Charlie moaned.

"You're taking the problem too seriously," Jill ad-vised. "You should relax and you might be surprised what will happen. Loosen up, Charlie." Listening to herself, Jill was amused to think she was giving such advice to a fellow at least three times her age. Yet if she didn't help Charlie in this delicate matter, who would?

Charlie peered at her. "Loosen up? Are you referring to the exercises we all do before the Senior Striders race-walk? I fail to understand how that—"

"No, not physical loosening," she said with a smile. "Mental loosening. Your thinking is too rigid, and that's why you're having problems with . . . with Gladys."

"Dear me, you may be right, but discipline and duty have been my code for more years than you can imag-ine. To cast off those restrictions at my age . . ."

"If you don't cast them off now, when will you?"

Charlie flushed a deeper crimson. "You see," he said, creasing the bag with his fingers, "I never expected to . . . That is, I thought never again to . . . Well, I really don't know about this. I could be inviting chaos."

"Chaos? Now really. Aren't you overreacting a little?"

"I must consider the consequences of my actions."

Jill hid her smile. She and Spence had to worry about consequences, but not Charlie and Gladys. Age did have its compensations. "I think you're being far too cautious," she said. "You deserve a slice of happiness, and you should take it."

Charlie rested his chin on his hand and stared into space. "I don't know if I dare," he mused.

"Dare."

"I wonder if she likes to travel?"

"Ask her."

He shook his head. "It would never work."

"That's negative thinking, Charlie."

"Of course, I don't recall anything in the manual that precludes this," he said, as if to himself.

"Manual?" She imagined him studying Masters and Johnson or *The Joy of Sex*. Poor Charlie. "Just do what comes naturally," she advised. "All the sex manuals in the world won't replace a loving touch by someone who cares about another."

He blinked. "Sex manuals? Who said anything about sex manuals?"

"I thought that's what you meant, when you said something about the manual didn't preclude something. And I want you to know that books can only do so—"

"I see what you mean," he said quickly, his ears pink. "And you're so right, my dear. I'll keep what you've said in mind. And now to a more important topic. . . . How is everything between you and Spencer?"

At the mention of his name, Jill began to tingle all over. "You haven't talked with him about . . . about us?"

"Not a great deal. But from the look on his face, I have hopes that you and he reached some sort of understanding last night."

"Um, I suppose you could say that." Jill busied herself cleaning up the debris from her lunch.

"Excellent, excellent. Certainly now you see the wisdom of staying through February fourteenth."

Jill looked up. "I do?"

"Don't you want to assure a future with Spencer?"

"I—I don't know. We've only just begun to—"

"You don't know?" Charlie frowned. "Then you're not as far along as I'd hoped. That's what comes of slacking off on the job, of course, of imagining that I can dally with a beautiful woman. I have no one but myself to blame."

"Why on earth do you keep insisting that what happens between Spence and me is somehow up to you?"

Charlie stood and picked up both lunch bags. "Because it is, my dear," he said, and left the office.

Jill stared after him, openmouthed. One minute Charlie was confiding his lack of sexual ability, and the next he was implying that he was in charge of her love affair with Spence. Dear as the old man was, he was also one pickle short of a jar. Perhaps she was wrong to push him toward Gladys, who seemed perfectly sane.

As Jill pondered whether to talk with Gladys about her beau, Spence walked into the office and sat down in the chair recently vacated by Charlie.

"Charlie just chewed me out," he said with a grin. "He wants a commitment that we'll be together on February fourteenth, and I told him I wouldn't be a party to interference with your plans. I described your map, and he said I had no business being intimidated by a thing like that. I told him about dinner at my parents' house tonight. He was pleased that I was taking you home to meet the folks."

"Spence, you didn't say anything about . . ."

"Our plans after dinner?" His gaze was gentle. "No, of course I didn't. That's our private concern."

"I should have known you wouldn't tell anyone, even Charlie. Did he say anything else to you?"

"No, he had to go—Gladys was waiting at the skating pond. But when he left I could tell he was still irritated with me for not being more assertive. Somehow I'm supposed to keep you here through the fourteenth."

She considered the situation for a moment. "Spence, do you think Charlie should see a doctor or anything?"

"M.D. or Ph.D.?"

"Maybe both. He's really acting strange about this St. Valentine's thing."

"I suppose, but so far it's all pretty harmless."

"What about Gladys? Does she know that Charlie is . . ."

"A little nutty? She knows. She told me that's one of the things that fascinates her about him. If some therapist got rid of all his little quirks, Gladys might not want him anymore."

Jill groaned.

"I wouldn't worry about Charlie, if I were you," he said, leaning his arms on the desk. "I've known him for several months, and so have Gladys, Robert, George and Bernie. Nobody's ever thought he was a danger to himself or anyone else. If he's a little cracked, it's a neat kind of craziness. All he wants out of life is to bring lovers together, and we could use a few more people fixated on that, don't you think?"

Jill gazed into his dark eyes. "When you put it that way, I guess so."

Spence glanced toward the office door he'd left open behind him. "Wish I could shut that," he said in a low tone, "but Stephanie and Horace already suspect something's going on between us. No point in advertising it. He reached across the desk and stroked her hand."

"No," she agreed, as her heart beat faster.

"Tell me about the bus tour. How are we doing?"

She swallowed and tried to remember what she'd wanted to ask him. "Old buses," she said finally. "All I can find are two old buses. The newer ones aren't available on such short notice."

"Then I guess we'll have old buses. Can you get them for Tuesday?"

"I think so."

"When it's arranged, why don't you call Robert about the catering? Then if you wouldn't mind designing the invitations, I'll have Stephanie or Horace run them off at the copy shop and take them around today."

"Okay."

"Tomorrow I'll leave Horace in charge here," he continued, "so we can map out the route of the tour. We can drive it together."

She realized he was planning to be with her for the rest of the weekend. And then what? After spending tonight in each other's arms, would they spend Sunday night the same way? And Monday night? And . . .

He touched the inside of her wrist. "I can feel your pulse beating. Pretty fast."

"I think . . . you'd better go back out there and finish whatever it is you're doing."

"Killing time until tonight, that's what I'm doing. My folks are excited about meeting you. Anyone who believes in the original mall concept is already a trusted friend."

"I don't have any fancy clothes," she said, remembering another problem she'd wanted to mention.

"Wear your jeans. We don't dress up around my parents' house. Don't forget that my ancestors were casual types who sold supplies to miners. My family hasn't changed much since then." He continued to move his finger lightly over her wrist.

The contact was electric, but Jill couldn't pull away. "All right, then. Jeans it is."

"You can leave here whenever the invitations are done. I'll pick you up about six at the campground."

"You won't have any trouble finding me?"

"With you I seem to have built-in radar. Besides," he added, smiling, "I doubt anyone else parked there has a map of the United States painted on their van."

"True."

"Charlie really is upset because I'm not making you stay until Valentine's Day."

"Does he think you could force me to do that?"

He circled her wrist with his thumb and forefinger and brought her hand, palm up, to his lips. "He thinks I could get you to do that . . . without force," he said, tracing the lines on her palm with his tongue.

She had trouble speaking. "But you . . . wouldn't try."

He gazed at her silently for a long moment before replying. "There are times when I wonder if I can help trying."

JILL DISCOVERED that she'd been right about the black Trans Am when Spence picked her up at six on the dot.

"There's so much I don't know about you," she said, watching him handle the powerful car. "You obviously grew up here, but I can't picture you moving right into a job at your parents' store."

Spence laughed. "Why not?"

"I don't know. There's something about you . . . Well, did you?"

"No."

"Aha! My instincts were right."

He shifted into fourth gear. "I'm glad to see you using your instincts."

"It's a recently acquired skill. I've been listening to other people for most of my life. But for the past seven months, they haven't been around, so I've had to listen to myself."

"Good."

"So what were you, before you became a shop keeper?"

"I flew a little."

"Flew a little. Come on, Spence."

He grimaced. "I was part of the war machine. That's why I cherish people like Charlie who would sooner die than carry a gun."

"A fighter pilot?"

"Yes."

"Figures," Jill said, watching the way he handled the car. "But fighter pilots don't get the job by accident. I've seen *Top Gun* and I know you have to work at making the grade."

"Oh, I wanted the job, all right. I'd always dreamed of flying, like most little boys, especially ones who grow up in Colorado Springs, almost next door to the Air Force Academy. I still love flying—in fact, I'm in the process of dickering for a little Cessna to have fun with—

but eventually I realized that I wasn't in the Air Force just to fly around. I was there to kill people, if the need arose."

"Witness our love," Jill murmured.

"What?"

"Oh, I was remembering what Charlie said your last name meant—'witness our love.' I suppose a last name like Jegger doesn't really fit well with bloodshed."

"Nope. Neither would Amory, if what Charlie says is right, and it means 'loving.'"

"He's right. I looked it up in the bookstore."

"Oh?" Spence seemed pleased. "Did you look up mine?"

"Yes, and Charlie's right about that, too."

"Hmm. I wonder if that means you'll do the loving and I'll watch." He grinned at her.

"Think so?" Jill felt rosy, warm and sexy—probably not the best way to greet Spence's parents.

He glanced at her. "No. I'm a lousy spectator. I prefer participation."

"Glad to hear it," she murmured. "And now I think we'd better change the subject."

He smiled. "It's a becoming subject for you. Your cheeks are pink as a baby's bottom."

"Oh? And what do you know about babies' bottoms?" She wondered with a little shock if he'd tell her about the children he'd had with his first wife. Jill hadn't even considered the possibility. There was so much she didn't know about Spence Jegger.

"Nieces and nephews. I'm the last of six kids and the only one who hasn't presented my folks with grandchildren."

"Oh," she said, adding his large family to her small cache of information. "How come none of your brothers and sisters are involved in the store?"

"Didn't want to be. I didn't think I wanted to run it, either, and the whole business would have passed out of the family when the mall was built. I got the news about the sale of the land while I was in Germany, about the time I had to decide whether to reenlist. I came home."

"With your wife?"

"No. She's German—didn't want to leave."

She studied his profile. "That must have hurt."

"No more than I hurt her, not loving her enough to stay." He shook his head. "It wouldn't have worked, anyway. She loves men in uniform, especially pilots, and I would have left the Air Force soon, in any case. I got a Christmas card from her and she's marrying a guy from my squadron this summer."

Jill wanted to ask if his wife's remarriage bothered him, but before she could phrase the question, he pulled up in front of a stately old two-story home.

"We're here," he said, turning off the engine.

She gazed in admiration at the white house with its forest-green shutters flanking each window. An ornamental iron fence ran the perimeter of the snowy yard, where twin blue spruces stood sentinel on either side of a freshly shoveled walkway. "That looks like a carriage house that's been converted into a garage," Jill observed. "Was this place built during the gold rush days?"

"Pretty close. My ancestors had to sell a few ropes and picks before they could afford to put this up, but yeah, the house has been in the family for almost a hundred years."

Jill glanced down at her jeans. "The house is quite elegant, Spence. I feel underdressed."

"Don't you dare," he said, squeezing her hand. "You look great. Come on, let's go in before you get even more nervous."

He guided her down the walk; roots from the tall spruce trees were pushing up under the cement, making it cracked and uneven. "Watch your step. My mother's sure someone will fall and sue us one day, but Dad can't stand to chop down the trees."

"I couldn't either."

"I figured as much," he said, giving her a gentle squeeze as they mounted the front steps to the porch, with its miniature Doric columns. He reached for the polished brass doorknob, but before he could turn it the door swung open to reveal a tall, smiling, gray-haired woman straight out of an L. L. Bean catalogue. Despite the formality of a chandelier hanging in the foyer and fresh flowers reflected in a gilt-framed hall mirror, Spence's mother was dressed in corduroy slacks and an oxford-cloth shirt under a pullover sweater.

"Welcome to our home, Jill," she said, ushering them inside. "Stanley will be down in a minute."

For a moment Jill thought she'd heard the words "welcome home," for that was the way she felt as soon as she stepped across the threshold.

"Charlie said we'd fall in love with you," Spence's mother continued, taking their coats, "and I think he may be right. Spencer, give your old mother a hug."

"Hi, Mom." Spence embraced her warmly, coats and all, before helping her hang them up. "What was that about Charlie?" he asked.

"He called here about a half-hour ago and asked if either you or Jill would call him back immediately when you arrive. I have the number right here." She reached in her slacks pocket and pulled out a piece of paper.

"Is anything wrong?" Jill asked, exchanging a worried glance with Spence as he took the paper.

"Didn't sound as if anything was wrong. He seemed quite cheerful. Staying with Gladys must be good for him. I never did understand how he could be happy all alone in the back of the store."

"I'll call," Spence said. "I'll use the phone in the office."

"That's fine," his mother responded with a grin. "That way Jill and I can talk about you while you're gone. Come on, Jill," she said as Spence left. "I'll give you the cook's tour of the downstairs. I'd take you upstairs, too, but Stanley's liable to be running around in his BVDs. He spent the afternoon chopping wood, and I told him it was getting late, but he wouldn't listen." She shrugged. "I should be used to it after forty-six years, but it still ticks me off."

"Forty-six years," Jill repeated, following her into the living room where a fire, probably thanks to Stanley Jegger's efforts, blazed on the hearth. "That's really great to be married that long."

"Some people might say we're simply in a rut. Look at us—same town, same marriage partner, same house, most of the same furniture," she said, waving a hand around the room at what looked to be priceless antiques. "We were even in the same business until two years ago."

"I envy you both, Mrs. Jegger. I'd love to find my niche and stay in it."

"Eileen," she said, surveying Jill with a careful eye. "Eileen and Stanley. You know, Charlie said some pretty wild things on the phone."

"Do I want to know what they were?"

"That depends." Eileen led her through a dining room sparkling with polished wood surfaces, old silver and crystal stemware. "How do you like the house so far?"

"I think it's lovely." Jill hesitated to admit her strong attachment to the house after such a short time.

"There's lots of upkeep to a house like this. I do hire a housekeeper, but you can't leave everything to paid help. The details require a loving hand—my hand. Some women might find that wearisome." She glanced at Jill.

"Taking care of a house like this and soaking up all the history would be a joy."

Eileen nodded. "Let me show you the kitchen."

After cooking on a Coleman stove for seven months, Jill was awed by Eileen's beautiful kitchen. Copper-bottomed pots hung from a rack over a wide butcher-block island, and the walls and floor were brick. Open shelves held the rest of her dishes and utensils. The aroma of roast beef came from an oven set into the brick wall, and vegetables simmered on the stove. "Wonderful," Jill breathed.

Again Eileen nodded. "Spencer will live in this house someday. None of the other five kids has any desire to move back to Colorado Springs, so he's the logical one to have it, considering that he's also taken over the business."

Jill met Eileen's gaze. "Exactly what did Charlie say to you?"

"I think you can guess. It had to do with you and Spencer."

"Mrs. Jegger—Eileen—Spence and I just met. Charlie's a romantic, that's all."

"He predicted you'd say that. He maintains that you are the right woman for Spencer."

Jill sighed. "Even if I were, I can't get serious about anyone until I have some idea what I want to do with my life. Charlie doesn't seem to understand that marriage is not a career choice."

"Charlie's from a different generation," Eileen said. "In his day, and in mine, marriage was a career choice for most women. And speaking of which, I hear my career choice coming down the stairs."

From the living room, a man's voice boomed out, "Where is everybody? Where's the party?"

"In here, Stanley," Eileen called.

Jill marveled at the pleasure on Eileen's face at the sound of her husband's voice. Forty-six years, and Eileen still loved Stanley. A picture of her counterpart—tall and gray-haired—flashed through Jill's mind. When Stanley arrived in the kitchen, she had to stop herself from staring.

Stanley Jegger was at least ten inches shorter than his wife, and round, and bald. But when he looked at Eileen, his expression held the same devotion as hers. He shook Jill's hand warmly and asked where they'd hidden his son.

"I'm here," Spence said from the doorway, and stepped forward to embrace his father. "I had a call to make."

"Is Charlie all right?" Jill asked. She couldn't imagine why he would have called unless it was an emergency.

Spence leaned against the counter. "Charlie is fine. He gave me a message for you—said to tell you he's learning how to loosen up."

"Uh, that's nice." Jill wondered what Spence's parents would think of a message like that. "He didn't call just to say that, did he?"

"No, he didn't. He wanted us to be the first to know. He and Gladys are engaged."

"Engaged!" Jill stared at him. "So soon?"

"It's not all that soon. They've known each other for several months. I think it's great myself. They want us to be maid of honor and best man for the wedding."

"Why, how nice," Eileen said. "When's the wedding?"

Jill could have told her. She couldn't believe that Charlie would stage a wedding ceremony just to fulfill his St. Valentine's Day prediction for her and Spence, yet it seemed that he might have done exactly that. She looked at Spence. "They're getting married on February fourteenth, aren't they?"

He nodded. "At eight in the morning, in the mall. He wants to know if we'll both be there."

"What did you say?"

"I said we'd let them know, that after all, you had planned to leave earlier than that."

"Can't see what difference a few days would make," Stanley said. "Spencer told us you have this trip sketched out and need to stay on schedule, but that little bit of time wouldn't hurt, would it? I bet it would make Charlie Hartman happy to have you two stand up for him."

"I'm sure it would," Jill said, still struggling with the news. Surely Charlie wouldn't go to such lengths to manipulate her into staying. Or would he?

9

DINNER WITH SPENCE'S PARENTS was thoroughly enjoyable. Jill shared so many interests with Eileen and Stanley that she had to keep reminding herself that they were both over seventy. Her beloved G.G. at eighty-two was spry of mind, but walked with a cane and suffered dizzy spells. These two, only a few years younger, still square-danced once a week and hiked in the mountains when the weather was warmer.

Inevitably, the dinner table discussion turned to the mall and Tippy Henderson.

"I understand her motivation," Eileen said. "She wants to make a name for herself with her corporation. It's tough for women in this field, and she's trying to prove that she can be as hard-nosed as a man."

"Hey, wait a minute," her husband objected. "That sounds like a female chauvinist remark. All the people who designed the mall originally, and who approved the free trolley, the melodrama and the museum, were men."

"I helped with the concept," Eileen pointed out.

"True," Stanley said, "but look at the people who are fighting this—Charlie, Spencer, Bernie, George, Robert. All men."

"Gladys and Jill," Eileen retorted. "And that woman Spencer told us about, the one who runs the candle shop, and—"

"Oh, all right, Leeny," her husband said, reaching across the dinner table to pat her hand. "Don't get your hackles up." He glanced at Jill. "Ever since she started subscribing to *Ms.*, life hasn't been the same around here."

"Ha! You read it before I ever get the chance," his wife said.

"So I can understand what's going to hit me next."

Jill loved watching them together, lovingly sparring and making up. Her own father's death ten years ago had deprived her of these scenes before she was capable of understanding them and incorporating them into her view of how marriage should work.

"Whatever Tippy's motives," Spence said, laying his fork on his empty plate, "we have to stop her. Jill has the bus tour lined up for Tuesday and about half the tenants have already said they'd come. I'll be the tour guide for one bus, and I'd like you to be the guide for the other, Dad."

"Of course. I wish I could do more than pay for the buses and be one of your tour guides. I wish I could afford to subsidize the amenities Tippy wants to eliminate." He sighed. "Leeny told me to keep some of the money from the sale in reserve, but I wouldn't listen."

"Don't berate yourself," Eileen said. "Each one of the kids made good use of their windfall. I don't want the free trolley rides to end, either, but I'm glad Bill and Sharon have a house, as well as Spencer. John's finally in business for himself, and little Erin, our future celebrity, has a grand piano and the finest teacher in Akron."

"And Jan's going back to school, and Ted's bought that fishing cabin he always craved," Stanley added. "I know, and I wouldn't take those things away, either, but I want the Remembrance Mall the way it was intended—a shopping community of the future."

"I think there's a good chance the tenants will rally to the cause," Jill said. "I've seen it work before."

"And your idea about forming them into a unit is excellent," Eileen said. "I'm delighted that you showed up."

Spence glanced at Jill. "So am I, Mom," he said, leaving no doubt by his inflection that his feelings ran strong for this woman he'd brought home to supper. "So am I."

"YOUR PARENTS ARE WONDERFUL," Jill told Spence as they drove away from the house.

"They liked you a lot, too. I almost couldn't get you out of there."

She hadn't allowed herself to think much about going to Spence's house after dinner. But his single allusion to his impatience sent a current of electricity through her.

"But I'm glad they like you," he said gently. "And that you like them." He shifted gears then and took her hand. "I'm not surprised, though. With you, everything seems so easy, so right."

She felt the pressure of his fingers differently, now that she was focused on what lay ahead. She remembered his touch on her bare skin, his lips moist against her breast. "But you are not the answer to my problem," she said, more for her benefit than his. "No matter how we feel about each other, I still have to know what I'm all about before I can—"

"I know. But since I can't give you that knowledge, I'll give you what I can and hope for the rest."

"What do you think about Charlie's wedding plans?"

"I'm happy for him."

"He wouldn't have arranged a wedding just to keep me here through St. Valentine's Day, would he?"

Spence glanced at her. "I think the ideas came to him at the same time. He knows asking you to be maid of honor is a perfect way to keep you here, but I'll bet he's also uncomfortable living with Gladys, perhaps engaging in some hanky-panky, without marrying her."

"You could be right. He even hinted to me about a problem with impotence."

"Impotence? I'm amazed that he'd discuss something like that with you."

"He sort of talked around it. He said he couldn't indulge in such matters, and I advised him to loosen up."

Spence laughed. "So that was the meaning behind his message to you. Well, that's probably the main reason for the marriage proposal, then. Charlie's an old-fashioned guy." Spence turned a corner onto a residential street. "He wants a wedding before succumbing to the pleasures of the flesh."

Jill quivered at his choice of words. Soon he'd demonstrate his exact definition of that phrase.

He squeezed her hand and released it. "The automatic garage-door opener's in the glove compartment."

She began to tingle; they were almost there. She fumbled with the latch on the glove compartment and finally extracted the door opener.

"Go ahead and press it," he said. "We're only a block away."

His house sat on the crest of a hill in a development of impressive homes on spacious lots. The exterior combined native rock and cedar shingling for an elegant yet rustic look. "So this is your share of the mall sale," she commented.

"Yep." He wheeled the car into the double garage next to a small Jeep. "Mostly as an investment and to escape apartment living. This house is nice, but it doesn't have a soul, like my parents' house."

"I never thought of houses having souls."

"Neither did I, until I moved around while I was in the Air Force and lived in several that didn't. That old house we just left was one of the things calling me back here."

"Your mother said it would be yours someday."

He turned to her in the darkened car as the garage door slid down behind them. "That's right. Incidentally, she took me aside when we were clearing the dishes and told me you fell in love with the place."

"I suppose I did."

"Don't you see, Jill? Don't you see how it's all working?"

"I see that I'm on a runaway train with Charlie Hartman as the engineer. I have to know where I'm going, Spence."

He opened his car door. "You will, in time."

"Easy for you to say," she answered as he helped her out of the car and guided her toward a door leading into the house. "You're not the person everyone calls Jill of All Trades."

"Forget them," he said, unlocking the door and leading her inside to the kitchen. "In fact," he said, unzipping her quilted jacket and easing it from her shoulders, "let me help you forget them."

"I'm so afraid of detours," she said. "My life has been filled with detours."

Spence tossed his coat down beside hers on the counter. "This is no detour." He cupped her elbows and drew her forward. "This," he added, wrapping his arms around her and angling his head for a kiss, "is an eight-lane interstate."

Her sigh served as agreement, and he proceeded with a kiss that transformed agreement to charged passion. She didn't understand how he could so easily throw the switch that released her inhibitions, but within seconds she was pressed against him with unladylike eagerness.

He lifted his head and smiled down at her. "I suppose I should ask if you want a drink or something."

"I suppose," she said, trying to catch her breath.

"Do you want a drink or something?"

"Or something."

"That's what I thought." He ravished her mouth until her legs were rubbery with desire. "Come on," he murmured against her lips. "I know a far more comfortable place for this than the middle of my kitchen."

"I hadn't noticed that we were uncomfortable," she said, breathing raggedly.

"Maybe not, but we sure are vertical." He took her hand and led her through the dining area, past a sunken living room and down a carpeted hall.

"This is really a very nice house," she said as he whisked her along.

"Too new, too unfamiliar. I've only lived in it for a couple of months. The place isn't broken in yet. I'm counting on you to help me."

"Does that mean what I think it does?" she asked as they entered a room dominated by a massive canopy bed created from bleached logs.

"What do you think it means?" He smiled down at her.

"That no other woman has . . . been in this bed, in this room with you."

"That's what it means," he said softly, taking off her vest and beginning on the buttons of her blouse. "Maybe that's one reason this house doesn't have a soul yet. Maybe you can help give it one."

"You're putting so much importance on everything, and I don't know if—"

"Shh. Yes, you do." He took away her blouse and gathered her into his arms. "Otherwise you wouldn't have looked so happy when you found out that I've never had another woman in this room. You know what we're about to share is special, and you don't want thoughts of me with someone else spoiling the way you feel tonight."

"Maybe you're right," she murmured, gazing into his dark eyes.

"And let me tell you the way I feel about tonight," he said, combing his fingers through her hair. "Strange as this sounds, I feel like a bridegroom."

Joy flowed through her, joy she had no business feeling. "Maybe it's all that talk about Charlie and Gladys."

"No. Charlie and Gladys have nothing to do with the way my heart's jumping around right now. Or the way my hand trembles when I touch you, or the light-headedness when I imagine lying beside you in that bed, or the anticipation of becoming part of you, at last." He caressed her nape with gentle fingers. "You know what some people would say about all that?"

She wanted, yet feared his next statement. "That you're coming down with something?" she joked in an attempt to forestall it.

He gazed at her silently for a moment. "All right," he said, swinging her up in his arms and carrying her to the massive bed. "We'll try this conversation again in a little while. I can see that you need more convincing."

"My shoes," she protested as he dropped her, running shoes and all, on the gray-and-blue patterned spread.

"I'll bet you know how to take off your shoes. That is, if you want to take them off." He set about undressing himself all the while watching her as she lay, bemused and uncertain, in the middle of his big bed. "Then again, maybe you want to try this with your shoes on. If you want to talk about new and different, that would be a first for me. Personally, if you want my advice, I'd take off the shoes, and the jeans, and the underwear. Less trouble that way, less danger of tearing something in the throes of passion."

She gazed at him in fascination as he stripped down to his briefs and reached for the waistband to pull those off, too. She knew from the bulge against the white cotton that he was fully aroused, and yet he talked to her as calmly as if he didn't much care whether she took her clothes off or not.

"This is my choice," he said, pulling off the briefs. "What's yours?"

He was so finely made that her throat went dry just from looking at him. The ache within her grew fierce. Slowly she nudged her shoes off and kicked them to the floor.

"That's a start," he said, approaching the bed. "What about the rest?"

She noticed the tremor that passed over him as she unfastened her jeans and pushed them over her hips. When she shoved them to the bottom of the bed, she heard him draw in his breath. Arching her back, she unhooked her bra, and soon that joined the crumpled jeans. Her panties were last, and she took her time. The hunger in his eyes was worth every drawn-out second.

At last she was as naked as he. "That's my choice," she said, and waited.

He swallowed. "You're more beautiful than I ever imagined."

She knew from his eyes that this wasn't a line; he meant every word. He was truly bewitched by her. The astonishing part was her willingness to believe that she was, for him, more beautiful than he could have imagined. His adoration did amazing things for her, awakened longings she'd never known before. "Now come to me," she said, hearing a new and sensuous note of command in her voice.

"With pleasure." He lay beside her, and it was she who reached out first, to explore and conquer, to seduce, although seduction was only a game, not a necessity. He closed his eyes as she ran nimble fingers over his chest, his thighs. When kisses followed, he warned her to go easy.

"But I'm having such a good time," she whispered. As she built his desire, hers grew. When she reached the part of him so perfectly designed to give her satisfaction, an uncontrollable ache claimed her. She wanted, wanted more than she ever remembered wanting. She stroked him, and he gasped and stilled her hand. Loving her power, she placed a kiss there as he moaned her name.

He buried his fingers in her hair. "You have to stop," he said, struggling with each breath and pulling her gently away. "Let me get—" He rolled to the side of the bed and opened the drawer of the nightstand.

"Now," he said, a moment later, moving between her thighs. "Now, Jill Amory, the woman who thinks she doesn't know her own mind. Let's find out if this makes any difference."

Her vision blurred as she gazed up at him and waited with pounding heart. He came to her in one swift movement, a bolt sliding home. She knew then. She'd always known, really, from the first glimpse of him. She'd known how he'd feel, locked within her, how he would penetrate her heart as surely as he penetrated her body.

"Yes," he murmured, kissing her, withdrawing just enough to push forward again and remind her how well they fitted. "And now for the rest." He grasped her hips as if to teach her the rhythm, but quickly the pupil became the teacher and she set the pace. Leader became follower as he moved faster in time with her urgent whispers.

So easy, she thought, *so easy when it's right*. She felt spinning colors within her, sensations that became white-hot, glowing like a ball of molten glass on a blower's pipe. She asked and he gave, gave until the whirling glass bloomed, and finally, shattered in a torrent of happy tears. Her sobs blended with his cry of release; her pliant body absorbed his shudders.

Later, he stroked her hair and dried her tears with a caressing thumb. "I think we're creating the soul of this house," he murmured.

"I think so, too." Her answer vibrated with emotion. "Spence, I'm not a cry-baby. Really I'm not."

"Does that mean what I think it means?" he asked with a smile.

"What do you think it means?"

"That Aaron doesn't make you cry."

"That's right. He doesn't. Didn't," she corrected. "And in case you didn't know, that's over."

"Yes," he said quietly.

"So I have to finish this trip on schedule, if for no other reason than to go back and tell Aaron the truth."

He smoothed her cheek and gazed into her eyes. "What is the truth?"

"That I'm not in love with him."

"That's not enough truth. He'll imagine that you still might be, given time."

"All the time in the world wouldn't make a difference."

"Why not, Jill?" he probed.

"Because he's never made me feel like this." She paused. "I have to tell him about you, don't I?"

"If you want him to understand, yes, you do."

"I guess Aaron was the detour."

He sighed contentedly. "I'm glad you found the right road," he said, and kissed her until, in a whirlwind of renewed passion, she forgot all about Aaron.

JILL SLEPT SOUNDLY the next morning. Spence shaved, made coffee and poured orange juice without her realizing he was out of bed. He interpreted her deep slumber as a sign that she felt secure here with him. Today he'd convince her to spend the next ten days here, instead of in her van at the campground. If he had only ten days, he'd make the most of them.

Picking up the juice glasses, he carried them into the bedroom. He was about to set one on the nightstand beside her when she opened her eyes.

She squirmed to a sitting position, pulling the sheet over her breasts. "Hi," she said, hastily combing her tangled hair with her fingers as he sat on the bed and put his glass beside hers. Her green eyes, soft with sleep, mesmerized him, and every time she moved he caught the tantalizing scent of a woman well loved. His body's response was swift.

"Goodness, you're fresh as a daisy, shaved and everything," she said, tucking the sheet primly around her. He smiled at her modesty, considering the direction of his thoughts. "I must be a wreck," she chattered. "I didn't even hear you get up. I was out like a light. Usually I'm up with the dawn. Usually—"

"A wreck?" he interrupted, unable to keep his hands off her. He drew the sheet from her breasts. "You've got to be kidding."

"I wasn't kidding," she said, reaching for another part of the sheet and trying without success to cover herself. "I need to take a shower, and brush my hair, and—"

"You need to be kissed again," he said, cupping her breast and nibbling her bottom lip. She wasn't used to waking up with a man, he concluded, or else she was used to waking up with the wrong man, some prude who thought sex should be sanitized.

"No, really," she said, pushing gently at his chest. "Won't this be more fun if I'm all clean, and my makeup isn't smudged?"

"You've been watching too many television commercials," he murmured, nuzzling the hollow of her throat. Damn, but she smelled good, and she tasted even better—salty and musky and all woman.

"I can't possibly be very glamorous to you in broad daylight, Spence. Let me—"

"You don't know, do you?" he said, lifting his head to gaze into her green eyes. "There's not a beauty salon in the world that can duplicate the pure sex appeal you have at this minute." He dug his fingers into her hair. "This is tangled because I tangled it, while we were rolling around together on this bed last night." His tone grew hoarse. "I love to look at it, to see you like this, wild and free, with all the evidence of what we've shared—to touch, to smell, to taste."

She stared at him in disbelief.

"You think I'm making that up?" He untied his bathrobe and took her hand. "That's what you've done to me," he said, holding her hand against his rigid flesh. "And I'm not letting you get all squeaky clean and spoil everything. I want you, Jill, every inch of you, just as you are."

She trembled and closed her fingers around him. "I didn't know."

"Now you do." Gently he removed her hand and took off his bathrobe.

"You're so different from . . ."

He smiled at her and eased her back on the sheets. "Good," he whispered.

He sensed her shyness and took his time, starting with the creamy skin of her throat and shoulders, the inside of her elbows, her wrists. He sucked on each finger and heard the uneven note in her breathing. She was getting there. By the time he reached her nipples they were wine-dark and waiting, rosebuds on snow. He took each one until he was dizzy with the pleasure and her skin was slick with her own moisture.

He heard her faint whimper of desire and chanced the next step, through the soft valley of her rib cage, over her flat belly. He prayed he'd done his work well enough as he kissed the damp curls above his destination. When she tensed, he feathered the inside of her thighs with his tongue and mouth while she moved restlessly beneath him. *Ah, so sweet*, he thought. If she only knew.

Impatience overcame him and he grasped her hips. She moaned, knowing what he was about, but he didn't stop, couldn't stop, once he'd tasted her. And then came her moment of surrender, when she opened to him with an abandon that dazzled him. Now he knew her, to the depths of her being. She'd trusted him with her darkest secrets, and he would never forsake her. Never.

He caressed her as long as the pounding need in his groin allowed, but at last he kissed his way back to her mouth. Made crazy by the scent and taste of passion, he fumbled in the nightstand drawer. The simple process took forever, but at last he was free to lose himself in her.

She needed very little to slip over the top, he only a fraction more. The impact was so powerful that it nearly left him unconscious.

He slumped against her, and words of commitment tumbled out of him in breathless confusion. He didn't care. She might as well hear what she'd be a fool not to know. No matter whether she stayed or left, no matter whether the St. Valentine's myth was true or not, one thing was sure. He loved her.

10

JILL DECIDED not to acknowledge the frenzied words of love Spence whispered to her that morning. Perhaps he could admit his feelings, plan for a future, but she couldn't, not yet.

They spent the day touring the city and planning where the buses would stop. No snow was predicted for several days, so they agreed on an outdoor buffet served in Garden of the Gods Park. Walking hand in hand through the park, admiring red rock formations laced with snow, they congratulated themselves on the novelty of their plan.

By evening Spence had convinced Jill to cancel her reservation at the campsite and spend the next ten days with him. She didn't need much convincing. The prospect of ten more nights in the roomy canopy bed making love to Spence beat the heck out of sleeping alone in her cramped little fold-down bed in the van.

On Monday she rode to the mall with Spence. He'd asked her to spend the day personally contacting all the tenants who hadn't yet responded to the bus tour invitation. Jill found it hard to believe, but only a few days into Tippy's new regimen the mall had changed from the happy place she'd first experienced.

The trolley ran nearly empty and its bell seemed more demanding than cheerful. With no melodrama sending delighted audiences back into the mall every two hours, the smile level of shoppers was definitely down in Jill's opinion. Shop clerks weren't smiling much, either. Tippy was slowly killing something really lovely.

In the middle of Jill's collection of acceptances and a few refusals for the bus tour, the Senior Striders rounded a bend and bore down on her. She waved as she recognized Robert and Gladys pumping in the lead. George wasn't far behind, and there was Bernie using his walking stick as if he were polling himself forward on a raft. Charlie, as usual, brought up the rear.

Jill decided to join Charlie for a turn around the mall. She had a bone to pick with him about his wedding plans. Fortunately Gladys was far enough ahead she wouldn't be able to hear what they discussed.

"Why, hello, my dear," Charlie said breathlessly as she fell in beside him. "Decided to take a bit of exercise, did you?"

"I decided to ask you what this wedding date is all about, Charlie." She hoisted her shoulder purse over her head so her arms were free to swing as she matched his pace. "It couldn't have anything to do with keeping me here until February fourteenth, now could it?"

He gazed at her in pink-faced innocence. "Only if you agree to serve as Gladys's maid of honor."

"You know I'd feel terrible turning down a request like that."

"I was hoping you would."

"Charlie," she said, lowering her voice, "I would hate to think that you asked Gladys to marry you just because—"

"Absolutely not!" Indignation propelled Charlie forward and Jill had to step up her pace to keep even with him. "I would never toy with a woman's affections in that manner. The very idea."

"Charlie, I didn't mean to insult you," she said, finding herself short of breath, too. These Senior Striders were definitely in shape. "But your decision seemed so convenient."

He slowed down and beamed at her. "Yes, wasn't it?" he said, puffing out the words. "When I thought of asking Gladys, I realized that you would have to stay for the wedding. The entire plan is absolutely perfect, unless..."

"Unless what?"

"Unless I'm overstepping my bounds with this marriage."

"I don't understand." Jill's breathing grew more labored as they whizzed down the upper level of the mall. Few electric carts shared the space with them today. People either wouldn't or couldn't make the necessary purchases in order to use them. "Why would this marriage be overstepping anything?"

"Well, it was simply never considered in my case." Charlie exhaled through his mouth and continued with his explanation. "It would be a first. I'm not certain the world is ready to deal with a Mrs. Charlie Hartman. Gladys can adapt, I believe, and she's already told me she's willing to travel, but then again... There's a precedent, of course, with Mrs. Claus."

"Charlie, you're making no sense," Jill said, panting. "Sometimes I worry about your mental stability when you talk like this. Who is Mrs. Claus?"

"The wife of an associate," Charlie said, taking out his handkerchief and mopping his brow as they churned along.

"Are you part of some secret organization?" Jill asked, alarmed by his terminology. "Charlie, what haven't you told us?"

He glanced at her. "Do I have your word that you'll remain in Colorado Springs long enough to take part in the marriage ceremony?"

"Yes."

"Then I suppose you can be told."

"Told what?"

"Charlie Hartman is only a . . . convenient alias."

Jill slammed to a stop. "Alias?"

"Yes." Charlie kept going. "Actually, my official title is . . . St. Valentine."

"What?" she screeched.

Several heads swiveled in the pack of Senior Striders, but the group kept marching forward.

"Charlie Hartman, you come back here and explain yourself!" Jill demanded.

Without breaking his rhythm, Charlie made a graceful U-turn and propelled himself back to her. "Do we have a problem?" he inquired, breathing hard.

"Not *we*, Charlie, *you*. Here you are about to be married, and you're saying things that will land you in a padded cell long before the ceremony, believe me."

"Ah." Charlie took out his handkerchief and wiped his face. Then he polished his gold figure-eight pin and returned the handkerchief to his pocket. "Apparently you don't believe me."

"Charlie?" Gladys said, hurrying over to them. "Is anything the matter? When I noticed that you and Jill had dropped out, I thought I'd better check." She turned to Jill. "You look a bit distraught, my dear."

Jill stared at her. "Since when did you start calling me 'my dear'?"

"Perhaps I've been around Charlie too long," she said, laughing. "Couples do pick up each other's speech patterns, you know."

Jill felt instantly protective of this sweet woman who was engaged to a crazy man. "Gladys, could I talk to you?" She angled her head toward a bench a few feet away. "Alone?"

Gladys glanced at Charlie. "Well, I don't know . . ."

"It's perfectly fine with me," Charlie said, a twinkle in his eye, "but before you inconvenience yourself, I should tell you that Gladys knows all about my identity. I had to inform her, of course, before I could propose."

Jill blinked. "Of course," she said, backing away and eyeing them both warily now. "Uh, so Gladys, what do you think of his claim that he's St. Valentine?"

"Naturally, I was quite surprised at first."

"Naturally."

"But when you have time to think about it, it explains so much about Charlie."

"Uh, why, yes, it certainly does," Jill said, edging farther away from the smiling couple. "Would you two excuse me for a teensy moment? I promised Spence I'd stop back at the store and let him know how the replies are going for the bus tour tomorrow. I'll catch up with you two later, and we'll talk about this some more."

"Certainly, my dear," Charlie said, nodding. "Incidentally, dress will be quite informal."

"Dress?"

"For the wedding ceremony. Everyone can wear whatever's most comfortable."

"Oh. Right." *In both your cases that might be a straitjacket*, she thought as she turned and fled down the wooden staircase. Racing through the lower level of the mall, she dashed into Jegger Outfitters, brushed past several customers and finally reached the safety of Spence's office.

He glanced up from the paperwork on his desk and smiled. "What a terrific—"

"They're both crazy as bedbugs," she gasped, closing the door behind her and leaning against it. "The only consolation is that they're too old to have children, so they can't breed more crazy people."

Spence stood and walked around the desk. "Who?"

"Charlie and Gladys. He thinks he's St. Valentine, and she believes him. She's ready to be the counterpart of Mrs. Santa Claus. I guess she'll serve him milk and cookies after he comes home from his round of match-making."

Spence laughed. "Come on, Jill. They're pulling your leg."

"I wish I believed that. I'm telling you, they looked deadly serious to me. I'm trying to figure out our responsibility in all of this. We can't just let them carry on with these delusions, but I don't know what to do."

"Why can't we?" Spence leaned against the desk and smiled. "I had a feeling Charlie believed he had some special mission to bring lovers together. Pretty creative, assigning himself the role of St. Valentine. I surely wouldn't have thought of it."

"Yes, but you're not a candidate for the loony bin, either. And what about Gladys? How can we allow some nice lady who once was sane to traipse around the countryside playing Cupid, or Cupidess, in this case?"

Spence folded his arms. "How do you plan to stop her?"

"Well, we could...there must be...I don't know. Can you help me out, here, Spence? I tell you Charlie and Gladys's brain just filed a Chapter Eleven. They're both on a very long lunch break."

"So?"

"So we have to do something."

He stepped forward and put both hands on her shoulders. "No, we don't. We have real problems to deal with. I've seen old folks hobbling around the mall today because they hadn't bought enough stuff to ride the trolley. The melodrama is shut down until further notice, and word is that Tippy the Lip is escorting the representative from Anderson's Department Store as if he were visiting royalty."

"But—"

"What real harm can someone like Charlie do? All he cares about is spreading love, and I can't argue with that goal. If Gladys wants to go along with it, she obviously has her reasons, and I wouldn't presume to tell a sixty-five-year-old woman her business."

"I suppose you're right," Jill admitted reluctantly. "Gladys is free to do whatever she wants."

He tipped her chin up with his forefinger. "We all are," he said, "in the long run. We all have to live as we see fit, not as someone else sees fit. I say let's leave Charlie alone to do his thing. After all, he worked hard to bring us together, and that wasn't all bad."

Calmed by his compassion and understanding, she gently traced the smile lines around his mouth. "Not even a little bad," she murmured.

"As long as the door's closed, and Stephanie thinks we're in here smooching, how about one for the road?"

"Good idea." She wound her arms around his neck and leaned against him.

"Oh, but you feel good against me," he said, rubbing his hands everywhere he could reach. "Maybe we can leave early today."

"Not unless I've contacted all the tenants we haven't heard from. We need to fill those buses."

"I'd like to fill something else right now," he murmured, pressing against her. "Come on, give me a good kiss and I'll force myself to let you finish your rounds."

She parted her lips and brushed his mouth in a playful gesture.

"You can do better than that."

"Yeah, I can." She cradled his head, enjoying the luxuriousness of his springy dark hair, and fitted her mouth over his. Slowly she ran her tongue across his teeth and gradually explored deeper until he groaned and tightened his arms around her.

She felt the increased tempo of his heartbeat, the arousal beneath his jeans. In a moment they might both forget where they were and begin plucking at buttons and zippers. Quivering, she drew back. "How was that?"

He took a long, shaky breath. "Not bad. I could suggest one or two areas of improvement, if you'd like to try again."

She smiled and stepped toward the door. "Save your suggestions for a little later."

"Spoilsport."

"Thanks for setting me straight about Charlie and Gladys. You're right. Oh, and dress casual for the wedding."

"Ours or theirs?"

She gazed at him, speechless.

"I know which one you meant," he said softly. "Just trying on the other idea for size."

"That idea's a little big for us right now, Spence."

"Yeah, I guess. Well, see you soon. We'll work on your kissing."

"Sure." She left his office wondering how she and Spence had moved so quickly from "Hello" a mere week ago to "Will you marry me?" or the equivalent thereof, today. Charlie might claim credit for it, of course. Charlie might say that's what happens when you're brought together by St. Valentine, and your last names mean "loving" and "witness our love." Spence's words from Saturday night marched forward, demanding her to acknowledge them. "I love you, Jill," he'd said; she'd tried to block them out, but they'd made a permanent mark.

She walked down the mall and slowly climbed the oak-and-brass stairs. "I love you, too, Spence," she murmured, safe in the knowledge that neither he nor Charlie Hartman could hear her admission.

ON TUESDAY AFTERNOON Jill sat at a linen-draped table in the midst of red rocks and scattered patches of snow and took satisfaction in the success of the bus tour. A moment earlier Spence's father had come by to congratulate her on an inspired idea. The tenants of the Remembrance Mall were having a great time eating Swedish meatballs, cold shrimp, various cheeses, barbecued chicken wings and bite-size pieces of tropical fruit. Robert had even instructed the caterer to provide plenty of red and white wine.

"I heard from Spence's father that this tour was your idea." Hedda Kramer, owner of the candle shop, approached Jill, balancing a full plate and a plastic glass of white wine.

Jill smiled and made room at the table. "The tour was, but one of the Senior Striders donated this little feast."

"How come none of them are here? They're obviously very involved in this situation."

"After what happened at the meeting they were afraid the tenants would resent having them around. In fact, maybe I shouldn't have told you where this buffet came from, but Spence told me you were friendly to the cause."

"I am, and I won't tell," Hedda promised, spreading a napkin on her lap. "And speaking of Spence Jegger—" she added, nodding toward a spot several yards away where Spence stood talking with a group of people "—he really knows some fascinating things about Colorado Springs history, doesn't he?"

Jill glanced fondly in Spence's direction. "I think he feels a responsibility to know the history, considering he's named after Spencer Penrose."

"I loved the story about Penrose driving his pet llama down Tegon Street to protest prohibition." Hedda lifted her wineglass. "Without men like him, we might not be drinking this today."

"Without him we wouldn't have the Broadmoor Hotel or the Cheyenne Mountain Zoo, either," added the optometrist, who had joined them at the table. "But my favorite story was the shoot-out with Kansas City Blackie at the gas station. The chase scene, with Blackie in his Marmon and the fire chief in his Stutz Bearcat, roaring up Nevada Avenue, and that crazy reporter, what was his name?"

"Ford Frick," Jill supplied with a grin.

"Yeah. What a name. Sounds made up. Anyway, Ford Frick hanging on the running board of the Bearcat. And then they stopped chasing Blackie because all they had for a weapon was a fire extinguisher. I love it."

"Did you know that Katherine Lee Bates wrote 'America the Beautiful' after standing on top of Pikes Peak?" asked someone from the end of the table.

"I knew that one," Hedda replied. "There's something about it in the Remembrance Mall museum."

"Yeah," the optometrist said, "and I guess there's something about Kansas Blackie in the museum, too. I never did take the time to go through the place, but I will now."

"Good," Hedda commented, spearing a Swedish meatball. "Then maybe you'll also sign the petition Spence drew up to keep the museum where it is. The shoe outlet space is far too small."

"Well, I don't know about that," the optometrist said, zipping his coat against the cold. "That petition also mentions keeping the trolley free, and the melodrama theater staying rent-free, too. Did you get that memo from Tippy?"

"What memo?" Jill and Hedda said together.

"It'll be waiting for you when you get back, I guess. I'm sure she sent one to everybody. She projects that with Anderson's coming in, a reasonable rent for the melodrama theater and making the trolley and electric cars pay for themselves, we can expect a ten-percent reduction in rent across the board."

"That's a projection, not a promise," Hedda said. "You won't get any ten-percent reduction. She can't pass on all the savings to us because her goal is to make more money for her corporation."

"And even that could be short-lived," Jill said. "I have a hunch that the more she disrupts the mall, the less people will shop there. I predict business will eventually fall off, and you'll have sacrificed some wonderful ideas for nothing."

"I don't know," the optometrist said, rubbing his chin. "I just don't know."

"Besides," Jill added, "isn't goodwill worth something? I was so impressed when I first got here and realized that the merchants of the Remembrance Mall cared about things like art and history and helping the handicapped."

The optometrist pushed his plate aside. "I don't know that we were given a choice. That's the way the mall was originally set up, and we could either take or leave it."

"So now you have a chance to make a conscious choice," Jill said, tensing. "You can strike a blow for—"

"Time to load up and go home," Spence called to the group. "Garbage containers are over by the buses."

Jill glanced at Hedda in despair.

Hedda shrugged. "You do the best you can," she said softly, as the optometrist picked up his plate and left. "Tippy's got them by the pocketbook, and that's a tender spot for many of us. I could use the rent reduction myself."

"But you signed the petition."

"Of course," Hedda said, gathering her napkin, plate and wineglass together. "And I have an eighty-seven-year-old neighbor whose greatest joy was riding on that trolley, plus a young friend of mine got some valuable acting experience at the melodrama theater."

Jill sighed as they walked toward the buses. "I just hope everyone who reads that memo from Tippy doesn't react the way the optometrist did. Did you see his eyes light up when he talked about a ten-percent rent reduction?"

"Yes. Of course he'll never see that, even if Tippy changes everything."

"But, Hedda, you wouldn't agree, even if you were guaranteed ten percent off your rent, would you?"

The candle-shop owner hesitated. "No," she said at last, "I guess not." She smiled at Jill. "But I'm a very noble sort of person."

"I'll vouch for that," Spence said, coming up behind them. "Hedda's one of the few people who signed a lease agreement because she wanted to be part of the unique concept. Right, Hedda?"

"Yes. I'm so wonderful."

"And modest," Spence teased. He glanced at the bus. "I think everyone's aboard but us. Ladies?" he said, making a sweeping gesture toward the door.

"I wonder if we should sing on the way home," Jill mused as they mounted the steps. "Singing builds comradery."

"And I wonder if the driver should start this bus," Spence murmured from behind her. "What's he waiting for? The other driver's already taken off."

"Maybe he's waiting for you to tell him it's okay," Jill said.

"Maybe." As Spence passed the driver he paused. "About ready to fire up?" he asked as Jill started down the aisle behind Hedda.

"Seems to be a bad connection in the ignition switch," the driver muttered, and Jill paused. "Can't get the damned thing started."

Jill retraced her steps to the front of the bus. "Uh, Spence, maybe he should radio the other bus. We'd be crowded, but—"

"Radio's broke," the driver said as he continued to click the key back and forth in the ignition. "I told them they shouldn't have let this buggy out of the garage, but someone needed it real bad, they said, so here we are. Stuck."

Jill groaned and glanced at Spence. "And the catering truck just left."

"Terrific." Spence peered out the front windshield. "And before too much longer it'll be getting dark. That's why I told everybody to saddle up."

The driver stopped turning the key and sat back in the seat. "Looks like you saddled up a dead horse."

"How far is it to the main entrance and a phone?" Jill asked.

Spence grimaced. "A ways. I'll get started."

"First you'd better tell them they'll be here awhile," Jill suggested, tipping her head toward the seated passengers, who were laughing and talking and hadn't seemed to notice the bus was immobile.

Spence swore under his breath. "I had hopes that some of these people would come around to our way of thinking, but this isn't going to help." He glanced at Jill. "No chance you could fix this thing, is there?"

Jill shook her head. "There are limits to my abilities, and working on an engine that size is one of them."

"Just thought I'd ask. Well, here goes nothing." Spence moved past her and called for everyone's attention. "As you might notice, the scenery outside your window hasn't changed much," he said, and got a laugh.

"What's the matter?" someone called from the back. "We stuck?"

"That's about it," Spence replied. "I'm hiking up to the entrance to phone for help. I'll get there as fast as possible, but you'll all have a wait, I'm afraid. I apologize for the inconvenience. Feel free to get out of the bus and move around, although it is getting a bit chilly out there."

"Any wine left?" asked someone else.

"The catering truck drove away a few minutes ago," Spence said, amid groans and boos. "Listen, I'm sorry to leave you all in this mess, but the sooner I take off, the sooner we'll get out of here. I'll see you all later."

"I'm going with you," said a man from the back.

"Me too," said another. "Beats sitting around here, since the wine's gone."

"Yeah, you're right," said someone else.

"Well, then I'll go, too," Hedda said, moving into the aisle along with the men.

"It's a fair hike," Spence warned.

Another woman stood up. "You wouldn't imply that the guys can make it but we can't, now would you, Spence?"

"Never," Spence said quickly, and Jill smiled. "But some of you have on high heels . . ."

"We'll make it," said another woman.

"Spence, they're all going," Jill said in amazement from behind him. "Nobody's staying in the seats."

He turned to her and shrugged. "Oh, well. You were the one who wanted to build team spirit. I guess this is it, huh?"

"I guess."

"Then let's get moving."

A few yards down the road someone started singing the dwarfs' marching song from *Snow White*, and as everyone joined in, Jill turned to grin at Spence. She mouthed the words "team spirit," and he grinned back.

The enthusiasm for their trek lasted through that song and the Marine Hymn, but few people contributed to "This Old Man," and by "The Ants' Marching Song" only a few diehards continued to shout out the words.

"So much for that," Spence said in an undertone to Jill. "By the time we get these folks back to civilization, they'll sooner boil me in oil than support my cause."

"We shouldn't have let them come on this hike," Jill murmured, glancing nervously at the disgruntled faces around them.

"There you go again. We couldn't have stopped them. They're all adults and perfectly capable of making decisions. The trouble is, I know what decision they'll make when they get back from this fiasco."

"I feel responsible," Jill said. "I suggested the bus tour in the first place."

"Don't blame yourself." He took her hand. "It was a good idea. I'm the one who said let's chance the older buses, and we had to do something fast."

"That's true. Wait until you read Tippy's latest memo. We must have left before it arrived."

"Do I want to hear this?"

"Probably not, but you'll see it eventually. She's projecting a ten-percent rent reduction if all her new programs go as expected."

"She's crazy. She'll never be able to do that and impress her corporation with added revenue at the same time. We can fight that piece of propaganda."

"Of course we can." Jill was glad to see his renewed determination.

From behind them someone stumbled over a rock in the twilight and muttered a curse.

Spence cringed. "Maybe we can fight it," he muttered. "And then again, maybe the golden age of the Remembrance Mall is over."

11

THE STRANDED TENANTS cheered up considerably after a newer, sturdier bus rescued them from Garden of the Gods Park and delivered them, at Spence's request, to a steak-and-ale restaurant for dinner.

"That was one expensive evening," Jill commented to Spence once they were back at the store.

"I didn't know what else to do." Spence sprawled on the bed and Jill sat in the easy chair in Charlie's old sleeping quarters. "I got those people out there and put them in a bad mood. The hell of it is, I'm back to square one with them. I don't have any more signatures on the petition than I had before the bus broke down." He sounded so discouraged that she didn't have the heart to offer some sunny contradiction or blithe reassurance.

"I'm sorry, Spence." She reached over and rubbed his ankle, the only part of him she could reach from where she sat. "We'll work on it."

"And that wonderful memo from Tippy the Lip. She probably found out about the bus trip and timed the memo to offset our advantage."

"We couldn't have done anything to keep her from finding out about the trip. But I can't imagine very many tenants will believe that ten-percent garbage."

"It confuses the issue, though, just when we need a united front."

"I know," she said softly.

"Damn."

"It's been a long day, Spence. I don't think we should try to solve anything tonight."

"But we have so little time. Anderson's could sign any day, and—"

"Let it go, Spence," she urged gently. "You need to put it aside, let your subconscious work."

He clenched and unclenched his fist. "You're right, but this is damn frustrating."

"I know," she said again, hoping to soothe him.

"I just—" He stopped and studied her for a long moment. "You're right," he murmured, levering himself from the bed. "You're absolutely right. I'll be back shortly. I think Horace must be about done closing out the register."

Jill watched him leave and wondered if perhaps she was more disappointed than he that the bus tour had ended, at least for half the tenants, in a stalemate. She wouldn't feel very good if she had to abandon him the following week with no solution in sight. Somehow she'd imagined that, with her ideas and Spence's determination, they couldn't fail.

As she waited for his return, she lost track of the exact time, but she gauged that at least ten minutes had passed and he still wasn't back. Balancing the cash must have taken longer than usual; all he needed was a discrepancy with the receipts to finish off his day, she thought. At last she heard his footsteps.

"Is everything okay?" she asked when he walked in.

"Everything's fine. Horace has left." He came toward her with a paper bag in one hand.

When he took a familiar box out of the paper bag she chuckled softly. "Bedroom supplies for later?"

"Supplies for now," he said, his tone husky.

"Here?"

"Yes."

"But . . ."

His dark gaze bored into hers. "We could wait until we're home, is what you want to say. But I don't feel like waiting, like being calm and civilized tonight." His tone deepened. "I need you now. Not later. Right now."

Her gaze locked with his as she rose silently from the chair, and he guided her backward until they toppled together onto the mattress. The springs squeaked under their weight as he plunged his tongue into her mouth and wrenched her blouse from her waistband.

Not bothering with the buttons, he pushed his hand beneath the material and behind her back to unsnap her bra. Excitement surged through her at his abandon, and the urgency of his kiss.

She started on the buttons of his shirt, but he pushed her hand down to the fastening of his jeans. She worked it loose and drew down the zipper. He was warm and full beneath it, already straining through the cotton of his briefs. She shoved the jeans and briefs over his hips and set him free.

With a muffled groan he withdrew his hand from her breast and fumbled with her jeans. He gave himself just enough access for what he wanted, and then his fingers moved swiftly, testing her readiness. "I needed you to be like this, all wet and wanting me," he said in a rasping voice.

He tore open the package he'd brought to bed with him, and with trembling fingers, she helped him put the condom on. She found the thought of making love here, in the center of this big, empty mall, incredibly erotic. Since the first night he'd pleasured her so thoroughly on this bed, she'd fantasized this scene. But without his boldness, she would never have dared make it a reality.

The old bed squeaked again as he drove into her, but she knew the shelves of boxes surrounding them would muffle the sound. Soon she no longer noticed the squeaks. The roaring in her ears, the pounding in her temples and the exquisite tension between her thighs drowned out everything else.

He kissed her, hard, as she began to reach a climax, and she dug her fingernails into his back. She hoped he was with her, for this was supposed to be for him, but she couldn't differentiate his shudders from her own. At last he lifted his mouth from hers, leaving her limp and panting.

"Did you?" she gasped.

"You bet," he said hoarsely, breathing like a marathon runner after a race. "And now...there's something else." He paused and took gulps of air. "The last time I said this, I didn't require a response. Now I do."

She guessed what was coming.

"I love you," he said, gazing down at her. "And I need to know how you feel about me."

She thought about what to say and wondered what sort of commitment he'd expect if she told him the truth.

"I feel love from you," he said when she didn't answer, "and heaven knows, when we're like this, I can't question your response to me, but I want to hear the words. Can you give me that?"

"I—I don't think it would be wise."

"Are you going to deny that you love me?"

"Spence, please, don't push for some declaration that would only make us both more miserable."

"Speak for yourself. Have I made you miserable, telling you how I feel about you?"

"You've put pressure on our relationship. I'm not ready for that."

He stared at her for a long moment. Then abruptly he left the narrow bed and went into the bathroom.

After he was gone she refastened her clothes, repairing the havoc he'd created with his impetuous lovemaking. He was angry with her, no doubt about it. But she'd warned him that she had to know herself before she'd make a commitment to anyone. To her mind, speaking words of love equaled commitment.

By the time he returned, she'd made a decision. "I'm moving back to the campground until Charlie's wedding," she said, standing.

His face contorted as if she'd slapped him. "No," he protested hoarsely.

"Staying with you isn't going to work. The more we're together, the deeper involved we become. I've known it was a mistake, from the beginning, but I—" Tears filled her eyes and she turned away.

He crossed the room and took her by the shoulders. "It is not a mistake. We're right for each other, just like Charlie keeps telling us. Look, I was impatient a while ago. I've warned you that impatience is a failing of mine. If you want the word *love* kept out of our conversation, then fine, it's out."

"But you were right to be impatient!" Her chin trembled. "I feel like a fool because I'm almost twenty-five years old and still playing butcher, baker, candlestick maker. I'm sick of indecision! Why can't I just make up my mind what I want to do?"

"Maybe you're trying too hard," he said desperately. "Maybe this deadline is spooking you. But don't shut me out, Jill. Stay with me, please."

She shook her head. "When I'm with you I forget about everything but us. The whole purpose of this trip is for me to be alone, to think, and staying with you is distracting me from that purpose. And let me tell you, I understand distraction. I'm a master at finding ways to sidetrack myself from what I know must be done."

"I don't buy it." He gripped her shoulders. "Maybe people have convinced you that's the way you are, but I've watched you work on the windows with creativity and efficiency until you finished. You attacked the mall problem with the same style."

"We still haven't solved it, either," she said, mustering the courage to look directly into his eyes. "You're wonderful, but I think better alone. If you'll drive me to your place, I'll take the van back to the campground."

Defeat began settling over his features. "What if the campground's full?"

"You know it won't be this time of year." She took a deep breath. "I have to go, Spence. I'll work with you on the mall situation, and I'll be the maid of honor at Charlie's wedding. That's all. Then I'll leave as we agreed I would."

His gaze was anguished. "Please don't do this. I feel as if you're slipping through my fingers. I can't let you go. Not now, not next week."

"You have to. It's the only way." She couldn't keep the tears back any longer. "You have to, Spence."

His jaw tightened. "If you leave town next week, and I don't hear from you by June twelfth, I'll come looking for you."

She shook her head, and tears spilled down her cheeks. "That wouldn't be a good idea. I'll come back if I can. You must know that."

"I keep telling myself that you will. It's all I have." He touched her damp cheek. "Except for Charlie's promise that our fate will be sealed on St. Valentine's Day."

JILL SPENT a sleepless night forcing herself to concentrate on the problem at the mall instead of her yearning for Spence's arms. She arrived at his office the next morning to find Charlie there with him. Spence looked haggard, but he smiled when she walked in. Charlie, on the other hand, sent her a disapproving glance, which she ignored.

"I've thought of a new strategy," she announced, sitting across the desk from Spence and next to Charlie. "Would you like to hear it?"

Charlie brightened. "Does that mean that you can rejoin Spencer? He said you had to be alone to think, but if you've finished thinking, then..." His optimism faded as she slowly shook her head. "Oh, dear I am most distressed by this turn of events. But Spencer assures me you will stay until after the wedding."

"Yes."

Charlie fingered the gold pin on his lapel. "Then I must be content with that, I suppose, but Spencer looks rather the worse for wear, wouldn't you say?"

Spence leaned back in his chair. "Thanks for the compliment."

"Well, of course you're still a fine-looking young man," Charlie added. "But I'd wager you had almost no sleep last evening, and I detect some dark smudges under Jill's eyes, as well. I don't believe this separation is healthy for either of you."

Spence glanced at Jill. "The lady has to have her space."

"Poppycock!" Charlie frowned at Jill. "My dear, I've tried to fathom this problem of a career choice, but—"

"Charlie, lay off," Spence interrupted quietly. "If space is what she needs, space is what she'll get."

In her gratitude Jill almost blurted out her love for him right then and there. "Thank you," she murmured.

"You're welcome." His gaze was steady, his smile sad. "Now what new strategy did you want to tell us about?"

"We need to call another meeting," she said, and briefly outlined her approach.

"Brilliant!" Charlie concluded when she'd finished.

"Sure makes lemonade out of our batch of lemons," Spence acknowledged slowly. "I only hope we can turn this thing around soon enough. Tippy the Lip has that Anderson's representative ready to sign the lease."

"How much time do you need?" Charlie asked.

"A couple more days—three, maybe," Spence said. "We can have the flyers out today, call the meeting for tomorrow night and possibly have the signatures ready to take in by Friday, if we get people stirred up enough."

"I'll see what I can do," Charlie said.

"About what?" Spence asked. "How can you slow up the Anderson deal?"

"Never mind how. Just leave it in my hands," Charlie said, pushing himself from the chair. "I'll report on my progress before the day is out."

Spence glanced at Jill and shrugged. "Okay, Charlie. Just keep it legal."

"My boy, I never run afoul of the law." Charlie paused. "Well, almost never. There was one time, in Arizona..."

Spence groaned.

"Don't trouble yourself, my boy. Everything will be just fine. You'll see." With a wave of his hand, Charlie walked out the office door.

"Thanks for defending my decision to go back to the campground," Jill said in a low voice after Charlie left. "That was a very noble thing to do."

He rested his chin on his hand and gazed at her. "Yeah. I'm noble, all right. I want to make love to you on this desk. How's that for noble?"

"Spence." She glanced nervously toward the partly open office door. "Someone might hear you."

"Doesn't much matter, if you mean Stephanie or Horace. They're sharp kids and they've already figured out what's been going on, or as of last night, not going on, between us." He leaned back in the chair and stretched. "So did you miss me?"

She watched the play of his shoulder muscles under his shirt. Did she miss him last night? Only with an ache that almost had her banging on his door at three in the morning. "A little," she said.

"But you got your thinking done."

"About the mall problem, yes."

"Anything else?"

"Not much else."

He leaned forward. "Come back to the house tonight, Jill. Shoot, if you're determined to leave next week, you'll have lots of time to think on the road."

She shook her head. "Staying with you would only make it tougher on both of us when I leave next week."

"I'm willing to suffer later for what I might gain now."

"That used to be the way I always operated," she said with a soft smile. "But this time I'm determined to think ahead."

"Just my luck you'd change your philosophy right now." He sighed. "Well . . ." He gazed at her silently until her skin prickled. "Then think ahead to this," he said at last. "You can be home before your birthday and back in my arms in time for a June wedding."

Her whole body tightened as she fought the urge to agree with him.

"I knew you wouldn't say yes or no, but I wanted to plant the idea in that busy mind of yours," he said. "I want you, Jill. Don't ever imagine that because I'm willing to wait, that I don't want you with everything in me."

The intensity with which he spoke made her tremble. She swallowed. "I'll keep that in mind," she murmured.

ON THURSDAY NIGHT Spence cornered Charlie and Gladys when they walked into the museum for the meeting. "Where've you two been all day?"

"Gladys and I spent hours in a florist shop, selecting floral arrangements for the wedding," Charlie said, patting Gladys's hand where it was looped through his arm. "I'm having trouble allowing her to pay for everything, I don't mind telling you."

"You're being perfectly silly," Gladys protested.

"Nevertheless, my dear, it wounds my vanity somewhat, being a kept man."

Spence smiled. "So get a job."

"I have one," Charlie said. "Unfortunately, it doesn't pay very well."

"Saints aren't supposed to care about money," Spence teased.

"Don't be flippant, my boy. I sense that you don't acknowledge my identity any more than Jill does. Thank goodness Gladys doesn't doubt me."

"Not for a minute," Gladys said, smiling up at him.

"I have to admit you do some amazing things," Spence said, "but I'm afraid calling yourself St. Valentine is a little off the wall."

"Which wall?"

Spence chuckled. "Never mind. Slang expression. Anyway, I've been looking for you today because Tippy the Lip called me early this morning and accused me of having something to do with Anderson's backing off for a few days."

Charlie exchanged a mysterious smile with Gladys. "What did you say?"

"I told her the truth, that I knew nothing about it."

Charlie nodded. "Good."

"She didn't believe me."

"Ah." Charlie tucked Gladys's hand close to his side. "Now you know how I feel, being disbelieved at every turn."

"Okay, I get the point. Besides, you obviously have something up your sleeve. How *did* you accomplish that delay with Anderson's?"

"If I told you, then you'd know, and the next time Tippy the Lip asked, you'd have to fabricate. I prefer things this way."

"You want me to believe in magic."

"Why not?" Gladys interjected. "I certainly do."

Charlie looked wise. Then he nodded in the direction of the museum entrance. "Direct your attention over there and tell me you don't believe in magic."

Spence followed Charlie's gaze and his eyes widened as he sighted Jill. "I do believe," he said reverently, gazing at the woman he loved. "But she had no business paying for new clothes, just to make this speech. That suit looks expensive."

"Don't worry, my boy. In addition to purchasing the wedding flowers, Gladys and I took Jill shopping. I'll wager Gladys had more fun than our Jill."

"I had a ball," Gladys said. "She reminds me of my daughter when she was a little younger. I can hardly wait until my granddaughter is old enough to enjoy shopping trips."

Spence continued to stare at Jill, who had come in with Hedda Kramer. The two women laughed about something, and Spence drank in Jill's buoyant beauty. "I've never seen her all dressed up before," he murmured. "In high heels, and everything."

Charlie beamed. "Quite impressive, I'll admit. When those shoes were invented, I wondered at the practicality, but they certainly do something for—" He looked at Gladys and reddened. "That is, they enhance the line of—"

"They sure as hell do," Spence agreed, amused at Charlie's discomfort in front of his lady love. "Jill is gorgeous in jeans, but in a skirt, and a soft blouse and the way the jacket nips in at her waist, she really..." He stopped, choosing not to put into words what he was thinking.

"Well said, my boy," Charlie finished with a wink. "And here she comes." Charlie waved as Jill headed in their direction.

"Lovely, simply lovely," Gladys said when Jill arrived. "Burgundy was the right color choice, after all."

"Thank you." Jill glanced shyly at Spence. "Gladys thought I might carry more authority dressed like this. She wanted to make a contribution to the effort."

"I think I have," Gladys said.

"Most definitely," Spence added, stuffing his hands in his pockets to keep from touching her. "You look terrific."

Jill adjusted her shoulder bag. "Feels pretty funny, wearing nylons and heels after seven months of jeans and running shoes."

"You don't look funny," Spence said, and noticed that Charlie and Gladys had drifted away to give them some privacy. "You look as if you were born to wear clothes like that. I can't get over how versatile you are. No wonder you have trouble deciding where to put your energies."

"Thanks." She gave him a brilliant smile. "That was a nice thing to say."

"I meant every bit of it. In fact, if you can give me a little of your time this evening, I have a few more comments along those lines . . ."

"The seats are almost filled," she said, laying her hand lightly on his arm. "We'd better start the meeting."

He glanced down at her fingers resting on his sleeve and then looked back into her eyes. She drew her hand away, but the color in her cheeks and the light in her green eyes told him that the brief contact had affected her as it had him. His heart raced and his body tightened with desire. The past two nights without her had been hell. He wondered how he'd last until June, assuming that he stood half a chance of her coming back to him.

He cleared the emotion from his throat. "I'll get things rolling," he said, introducing her with pride and a splash of jealousy, as he watched other men in the room warming to her. It wasn't only the men, however. The women liked her, too. If he'd been smart enough to use her as a spokesperson before, perhaps they'd be closer to the goal.

She could do anything she chose, he thought as she began her speech. Was that her problem, that she had too many options? For one selfish moment he wished she'd been born with only one straightforward ability that pointed her in a single career direction. But then she wouldn't be the multifaceted woman he loved.

"Are all of you from the second bus recovered from our glorious hike?" she asked, and was greeted with groans and laughter. "Great. You'll be happy to know that the bus company offered to donate that vehicle to the museum, as an example of an ancient mode of transport."

Spence chuckled. She was clever, all right.

"But that isn't why I asked Spence to call another meeting," she said. "I asked for this chance to talk to you because our accidental hike through Garden of the Gods started me thinking. We've put a lot of emphasis on saving the museum, and I still believe in that. I'd also like to see the melodrama continue as free entertainment and a training ground for young Colorado Springs actors."

Spence noticed some nodding, mostly from people who had already signed his petition. Many people, mostly those from the second bus, sat with their arms folded and skeptical looks on their faces.

"But frankly," Jill continued, "the museum and the melodrama aren't the most critical elements of the Remembrance Mall. Remember what it was like for us, trudging along that road toward the park entrance, many of us handicapped by having the wrong shoes for that sort of activity?"

They were starting to get it. Spence saw the light dawning on several faces.

"They say you can never understand another's problem until you walk a mile in that person's shoes," Jill said, looking carefully around at the group. "On Tuesday afternoon we were given a chance, purely by accident, to experience what it might be like for a handicapped person to make the trip through this mall." She paused, and the room was perfectly quiet. "That's all I have to say," she added, and sat down in the front row where Charlie and Gladys had saved her a seat.

12

SPENCE WALKED to the front of the room. Jill had set the crowd up beautifully. He could tell from their open posture and their listening attitude that they were thinking, not merely reacting to Tippy's suggestion of fewer services and more revenue.

"I can't speak for the rest of you," he began, "but coming to work every day at the Remembrance Mall used to make me feel pretty good about myself. There was an atmosphere of goodwill. I don't know exactly how that translates into dollars and cents—it's tough to put emotion on a ledger sheet. But have you ever noticed that none of us has trouble hiring clerks? Help Wanted signs stay in the window an average of two days around here."

"Not anymore," commented someone from the middle of the crowd.

"My point exactly," Spence continued. "The atmosphere of goodwill is going sour. I don't feel the same pride coming to work that I once did. The melodrama's ended its run, and that place used to give me a lift. I don't see smiling, gray-haired folks enjoying the trolley these days, just grim shoppers who've managed enough purchases to afford the ride. In fact, I don't see many shoppers smiling, period."

"I'll smile when I get that ten-percent rent reduction," said the same belligerent man who always sat in the back.

Another man, young and hesitant, stood up and adjusted his tie. "Can I say something?"

Spence nodded. "Sure."

"I was on that second bus, and I'd worn new shoes that day. The unexpected walk was misery. I have the blisters to prove it." A few people nodded in sympathy. "What you guys say makes sense," the young man continued. "I don't feel the same coming to work since the changes started. I see a difference in my customers, too. I don't know about the ten-percent reduction—it may or may not happen—but the atmosphere of the mall is important. I think we have to put things back the way they were." The young man sat down amid murmurs of agreement.

"Thanks," Spence said. "I have one more thing to say. We've had these special features, but until now they haven't been used much at all in advertising. What if we suggest a campaign to the mall management, using the features as a selling point? Instead of cutting out the extras, why not use them as promotion tools to bring in more business?"

"You gonna put that in the petition?" asked someone.

"Sure, unless somebody objects." Spence surveyed the room. "Then it's in. Basically, that's all I have. The petition's here, if anyone wants to sign tonight. If you want more time to think about it, the petition will be available in the store all day tomorrow."

"What about Anderson's?" asked a woman.

"They've decided to postpone their decision until Monday," Spence replied, glancing at Charlie. "I figure we've got to hit Tippy Henderson with this petition tomorrow afternoon, and we need eighty-five or ninety percent of you to make it effective. We now have about forty percent. So unless anyone else wants to speak, we'll adjourn. The petition's on the table by the door."

Chairs scraped as everyone stood and started out of the room. Spence walked over to where Jill, Charlie and Gladys waited for him.

"Well done, my boy," Charlie said, reaching up to pat Spence on the shoulder. "You and Jill make a fine team."

"We might get them this time." Spence smiled at Jill. "And you're right, Charlie. Jill's creative ideas have made all the difference."

"I don't know if we've got them or not." Jill glanced at the petition table. "A lot of people are walking out without signing."

"Yeah, but I saw the expressions on nearly everyone's face when you talked about what it must be like to be handicapped and have to negotiate a gigantic mall like this one," Spence said. "They'll be at the store tomorrow if they don't sign tonight. I just hope Tippy the Lip doesn't throw the petition back in our faces tomorrow afternoon."

"Surely she wouldn't do that," Gladys said.

"She has no legal obligation to abide by the wishes of the tenants," Spence replied. "And she's one stubborn lady, but I can't picture her standing firm against a petition for ninety percent of us. Let's hope we get that many."

"Let's hope so," Charlie said. "Well, Gladys, my dear, shall we be off?"

She smiled and took his arm. "We'll be back tomorrow," she said to Spence and Jill. "Senior Striders' walking day, you know."

"And we'll be checking on your progress with the petition," Charlie added. He glanced from Spence to Jill. "You two have a lovely evening."

"I'd better be going, too," Jill said, reaching for her coat on the back of the chair.

Reflexively Spence put his hand over hers. "Wait a minute. I thought maybe we could—"

"I'm afraid not," she said softly, giving him a look that pierced him through with longing. "I'll walk out with Charlie and Gladys."

He watched her leave. The high heels added a graceful sway to her walk, and he almost groaned with frustration. He'd have to let her go this time. No point in making a scene in front of everyone. But he reached a decision as his gaze traveled over her luxuriant hair, small waist and inviting hips. Before this was over and she drove away, perhaps forever, he'd make love to her once more, somehow, somewhere. He wanted one more memory of her body closing around him. And he needed to remind her, one last time, of their passion.

ON FRIDAY AFTERNOON at four o'clock, Spence's office overflowed with people wanting to accompany him when he gave Tippy Henderson the petition. Jill was squashed into one corner of the room with Charlie, Gladys, Bernie, George and Robert.

"Too bad we didn't get the ninety percent Spence wanted," George said. "With only seventy-two percent of the tenants on that list, Tippy may not go along."

"Seventy-two percent is still a clear majority," Bernie said. "Anyway, we have to go with what we've got. Time is running out."

"Okay, listen up," Spence said, speaking above the murmur of voices. "We can't all fit in Tippy's office, so I'll have to pick four people to go with me. There's nothing wrong with the rest of you waiting out in the hall, though, as moral support. I'd really appreciate that."

"So who's going?" asked someone.

"Jill Amory, because she's worked on this from the beginning, and—"

"That's okay," Jill demurred. "I don't need to go."

"Yes, you do," Spence said, with a glance that told her he'd make an issue of it if she refused. "This has been your project."

She flushed as most of the room's occupants turned toward her. "All right," she said quietly. "I'll go."

With a nod, Spence turned toward the others. "And Hedda Kramer, for her encouragement, and Tom Jorgenson, who spoke up in the meeting last night and changed some minds, I think. And a representative from the Senior Striders. How about Robert?"

Robert adjusted his glasses. "I think you'd better take Bernie."

"Oh?"

"Yes. He, um . . . well, just take him, that's all."

"Is that okay with you, Bernie?"

Bernie gripped his walking stick and glanced around at the group. "That's just fine with me. Let's get this show on the road."

"Surely Bernie won't try to charm Tippy now?" Jill whispered to Robert as everyone began edging out the door.

"I don't think *charm* is the right word," Robert said.

"Then what on earth . . . ?" Jill stared at Robert.

"Never mind that," Robert said, "let's go."

"What's all this about Bernie having to be the representative?" Spence asked when he reached her side.

"Robert wouldn't tell me," she replied. "Are you worried about it?"

"Charlie assured me not to worry. Whatever the secret is about Bernie, Charlie's not telling, either. For all I know we have Bernie, the Patron Saint of Shoppers in our midst. After Charlie managed to get Anderson's to back off, I'm willing to believe anything these old guys tell me."

"I still wonder how he did that," Jill said.

"Me too, but magicians don't reveal their tricks, I guess. It worked, whatever he did."

"Let's hope this does, too," Jill said. "Have you noticed we're gathering more store managers and owners along the way?"

"Yep. Tippy's got to be influenced by this show of force."

"And if not, we have Bernie, our secret weapon."

"Right." Spence grinned. "You know, I'm having fun. After all those years in the military, it's a blast to challenge authority for a change."

Jill laughed. "And what will you do when this is over? Find another cause to champion?"

"Maybe." He glanced at her. "If I could count on my sidekick."

She remained silent.

"Weekend's coming up, Jill. Any plans?"

"I'll be washing my hair."

"I'd love to help," he said.

"Spence, let's not go through this again."

He sighed. "All right."

Privately she wondered how she'd get through the weekend, but she had to, somehow. Charlie and Gladys would be married on Tuesday morning, and she'd promised to be there. Immediately after the wedding, she'd leave.

Before the crowd reached Tippy's outer office, Tippy's secretary appeared in the doorway and peered out. "My goodness," she said, her eyes wide. "What's all this?"

"We have a petition to present to Tippy Henderson," Spence said.

"All of you?"

"Yes, but only five of us need to talk directly with her. Will you tell her we're here?"

"I'll tell her," the secretary said, backing toward Tippy's office door. In a moment she returned, still wide-eyed. "You may go in," she said, edging sideways toward her desk.

Spence ushered the women in ahead of the men, so Jill was the first person in the office. Tippy sat behind her desk, smiling as if about to receive a commendation.

"So, Spencer Jegger, you finally got all your little ducks in a row," she said when Spence came forward and handed her the petition. She placed the papers on her desk without looking at them. "Now that you've delivered the results of this temper tantrum, you may all leave."

Jill's mouth dropped open in disbelief at the woman's rudeness. Tippy the Lip was aptly named. Jill wondered how she'd earned a position of authority, but perhaps she didn't adopt this attitude with her superiors.

"Before we leave, we demand a reply to our request," Spence said, his gaze threatening. "The majority of your tenants are unhappy, Ms Henderson. I suggest you consider what they have to say."

Tippy glanced through the pages of signatures. "In the first place, a fair number of tenants didn't sign this petition, and in the second place, they'll all sing a different tune when they receive their first rent reduction."

"And when will that be?" Hedda Kramer said. "Exactly?"

"I can't give you an exact date," Tippy said with a cool glance. "Once Anderson's is in, we'll have a better idea about that."

"We really don't care about the rent reduction," the young man named Tom said. "We want the mall back the way it used to be."

Tippy clucked her tongue. "Such reactionary behavior is a shame in someone so young, Mr. Jorgenson. And if you run that store on ideals instead of clearheaded business practices, you'll find yourself in big financial trouble."

"And if we lose our ideals," Spence said, "we're in trouble that can't be measured. Did you even look at the proposal for the ad campaign? Instead of eliminating our services for the handicapped and aged, why not use them as a promotion?"

"Because I don't care to," Tippy said, folding her arms on the desk. "An ad campaign would take money, which we may or may not recoup through increased business. My methods are much quicker."

"And deadlier," Spence said, his jaw tight. "I'm warning you that—"

"May I say something?" Bernie stepped forward and planted his walking stick beside him with a thump.

"And who might this be?" Tippy said, looking amused. "One of the erstwhile Senior Striders?"

"Correct," Bernie said, extending his hand over the desk. "I don't believe we've had the pleasure of meeting, Ms Henderson. My name is Bernard Bredvold."

Tippy's expression registered surprise for the first time. "I've heard that name."

Bernie released her hand and smiled. "That's possible. I used to play golf regularly with Clinton DeVeney."

Tippy blinked. "With Mr. DeVeney?" she said faintly.

"Correct," Bernie said again. "The CEO of your corporation, Ms Henderson. Clint and I go back a ways. Matter of fact, we graduated from Harvard Business School together."

"I see." Tippy looked dazed.

Jill watched in fascination. She'd suspected George, Bernie and Robert of being retired executives, but she hadn't pictured any of them this highly placed. Now she understood why Bernie had been sent to this office, but she also wondered why the campaign had been necessary, at all. Bernie was about to clean Tippy's clock with a few well-chosen threats.

"I haven't talked with old Clint in a while," Bernie said, eyeing Tippy carefully. "Thought I'd give him a call this weekend, find out how his golf game is. He promised to come out and see me this summer so we could play a few rounds at the Broadmoor."

Tippy nodded like a robot.

"I'll give him your regards, if you like," Bernie said.

Tippy nodded again.

"I'll tell him how thrilled you are with the free trolley system, and the museum and the melodrama here at the Remembrance Mall. Clint is a real fan of things like that."

Tippy made a noise in her throat that sounded like a suppressed moan.

"So," Bernie concluded, glancing around at the others in the office, "does that about wrap things up?"

"I'd say so," Spence replied. "We'll let you get back to work now, Ms Henderson."

Tippy didn't answer as they filed silently out of the office and past the secretary.

When they reached the mob of people in the hall, Spence held up two fingers in a victory sign, and the group went wild. "Come on," yelled someone, "I feel like taking a ride on the trolley!"

The majority of the crowd followed, but the four who had witnessed Bernie's performance in Tippy's office stayed behind. Joined by Charlie and Gladys, the group surrounded the tall, grinning man.

"Why didn't you tell us about this before?" Spence demanded. "You could have saved us a heap of trouble."

"Two reasons," Bernie said. "When I was president of my own company, I always tried to let people work out their own problems before stepping in. This experience was good for you, and now the mall tenants are far more united and ready for the next crisis, which will eventually arrive, I can promise you."

"I guess that makes sense," Jill said, "but what was the second reason?"

"Him," Bernie confessed, jabbing his walking stick in Charlie's direction. "I told him about my connection a long time ago, but he said this campaign against Tippy would help bring you and Spence together. I couldn't jump in and alter the course of true love, now, could I?"

Jill flushed and glanced at Spence. "I guess not," she said, and saw the light of hope flicker in Spence's eyes. "Anyway, thanks for saving the day, Bernie."

"I'm beginning to put this all together," Spence said. "Were you by any chance the one who convinced Anderson's to hold off renting the museum space?"

"No, that was George," Bernie said. "Charlie told us about the problem. George also had misgivings about interfering, although his sister-in-law owns a controlling interest in the Anderson's chain. All three of us— George, Robert and I—wanted to keep a low profile and only help if the situation got out of hand. When I heard Tippy the Lip in there this afternoon, I figured the situation was definitely out of hand. I may tell Clint to get rid of that gal, after all. She's horrible."

"I'd give her another chance, Bernie," Charlie said. "If you allow some of the atmosphere of the Remembrance Mall to influence her, perhaps she'll discover the joys of philanthropy yet."

"I wouldn't count on it," Bernie said, "but I guess we can give it a try. She could start by waiving the fee she's charging you and Gladys to hold the wedding in the mall."

"I imagine we won't be billed," Charlie said with a wink.

"Yeah," Bernie agreed, "but not because of Tippy's generosity. Take away that sword I've just hung over her head, and she'll be the same nasty, bullheaded—"

"Now, Bernie, my good man, don't be so hard on Tippy," Charlie interrupted. "Wait until she samples the rewards of being cooperative."

"You always believe people will come through in the end, don't you, Charlie?" Bernie replied.

"Of course," Charlie said. "Because they always do."

Jill could feel Charlie's penetrating stare, but she refused to look at him.

Spence turned toward her with a smile. "Ready to celebrate our victory?"

Agreement was on her lips, but she stopped herself. "I think I'd better get back to the campground," she said, and before he could answer, she turned and fled down the mall, away from temptation.

JILL SPENT Saturday and Sunday trying to forget Spence by playing tourist. G.G. would appreciate it, she told herself, and anything was better than sitting at the campground for two days. She doggedly covered the Air

Force Academy, the Will Rogers Shrine of the Sun, the Cheyenne Mountain Zoo, and the North Pole amusement park. Unfortunately the city's attractions had become thoroughly linked with Spence in her mind; he might as well have been with her the entire weekend.

Finally, after exhausting herself for two days, she prepared a simple meal on Sunday night and got ready to turn in early. A light snow was falling outside her camper, and she bundled into her warmest nightgown. She wished that she had the long johns she'd lost the nerve to select at Jegger Outfitters the night she'd chosen her other merchandise.

With a sigh she picked up a thick paperback novel, intending to try reading herself to sleep. The technique hadn't worked very well in the past few nights, but she hoped tonight it would. She was halfway through the first chapter when someone knocked at the door of her camper.

Edging back the curtains, she saw Spence, snow dusting his hair and the shoulders of his jacket. He was holding a large box and gazing up at her in silent appeal. She knew she shouldn't let him in, knew what would happen if she did. But she jumped barefoot to the floor of the van and unlocked the door.

He climbed in and filled the small space, leaving her no room for hesitation, no time to push him away before he hauled her into his arms and kissed her with snow-damp lips. His nylon jacket crackled between them as she clutched his sleeves made slippery with snow. The cardboard of the box he still held in one hand pressed against her back; the cold from his jacket penetrated the flannel of her nightgown, but she didn't care. His mouth was a remembered haven, his tongue a welcome delight.

"You taste of beer," she whispered between kisses.

"Bachelor party for Charlie," he said, dropping the box on the driver's seat of the van. He unzipped his jacket and nestled her against the soft velour of his shirt before claiming her lips again with a murmur of satisfaction.

He wasn't going to ask politely for this, she realized. He didn't plan to give her the option of saying no. If she wanted to put an end to his caresses and send him on his way, she'd have to do it now. Instead, her arms slipped inside his jacket, and her mouth opened to his exploring tongue.

He gripped her bottom, bare under the flannel, and guided her until she fitted tightly against the swell in his jeans. He lifted his head and gazed down at her. "One for the road," he said softly, releasing her slowly and taking off his jacket.

She made a feeble attempt at protest. "You shouldn't be here," she said as he began unfastening the buttons at the neck of her gown. "You shouldn't be doing this," she added as he gathered up the hem of her gown and pulled the garment over her head.

"But I will." He cupped her breast, cradling the nipple in the curve of his thumb. "I will," he repeated, arching her backward across his arm and leaning down to draw the hardened tip into the warm circle of his lips.

The heat of her response banished the chill from the small van. Every beat of her heart seemed to echo in the moist center that awaited him. She tangled her fingers in his dark hair, still damp from the snow, and closed her eyes to savor the coaxing pleasure of his mouth, as she would savor each step of his seduction. After tonight, nothing was certain. She might never know his lovemaking again.

With nibbling kisses he mapped the region of her breasts, leaving no part unloved. "You're getting pink all over," he praised, easing her upright and stepping back to admire his handiwork.

"You show no mercy, do you?" she said, breathless from the journey of his mouth over her skin.

"None." He pulled off his shirt and nudged off his shoes. Movement was restricted in the small space, but he took off the rest of his clothes with surprising agility.

"You operate well in close quarters," she said, glorying in the magnificence of his aroused body.

He guided her back onto the narrow bed. "I work with what I'm given," he said, kneeling beside the bed and running his palms over her breasts and stomach.

"Come here," she begged, gripping his arm and urging him to lie with her.

"In a minute." He caressed the inside of her thighs. "In a minute. I'm taking pictures for a mental scrapbook. You have beautiful knees," he murmured, stroking downward and placing a kiss there.

"That's . . . silly," she said, trembling as he gently bent her leg and kissed the inside of her knee.

"And toes." He traced each one with a feathery touch. "And...other parts," he said, his gaze sweeping back up her body.

She started to straighten her leg, for its position had left her open and vulnerable to him, but he pressed against her thigh with one broad palm. "Still memorizing," he said, his eyes dark with passion.

"I'll have no secrets," she murmured.

"That's the idea," he said.

Once he began his sweet assault, she was helpless to deny him. Dimly she recognized his motive for loving her so completely here, in this place where she would live for several months. After tonight she wouldn't be able to sleep in this bed without remembering the touch of his hands, his mouth.

"I know..." she gasped, "what you're...doing. You don't want...me to forget."

"That's right." He kissed his way back to her mouth. "You admit you're easily distracted."

"I can't imagine forgetting you," she whispered, gazing into the dark glow of his eyes.

"I love you."

She dared not respond. If she admitted her love, she'd never leave, never finish her journey.

"I can read your mind, you know. You're not hiding anything."

She stared up at him, silent and trembling. "Just love me," she murmured at last. "Let me feel you inside me once more."

Quietly he sheathed himself and moved between her thighs. "I want you to remember all of this," he said, holding back. "The moment before, when we each want the other so much we ache."

"I will."

"And how you feel with the first...mmm...the first thrust." He stayed very still within her.

She could feel the hammering of his heart against her breast and smell the pungent combination of his desire and hers. "Yes." She tightened around him and pushed her fingers into his back.

"And then—" He moved now, pressing rhythmically in the way he knew would drive her over the edge. "This," he said through clenched teeth.

"Yes," she gasped.

"Remember me, Jill. Remember me," he demanded, pumping cries of ecstasy from her until she arched upward in a quivering climax. Only then did he allow the spasms to envelop him, too.

13

SPENCE LEFT THE SMALL BED soon afterward. He dressed with the same economy of movement as he'd undressed, while Jill lay wrapped in the misty haze that always followed Spence's lovemaking.

Once he paused, and his gaze traveled over her uncovered body. "Come home with me," he said. "Marry me. We'll have the routine down pat after Charlie's wedding."

"No," she murmured. "I can't."

He didn't speak again until after he'd put on his jacket and was ready to leave. He leaned down and caressed her cheek. "I'm afraid you'll have to get up so you can lock the door behind me."

Nodding, she reached for her flannel gown on the floor.

"Here," he said, picking up the box on the front seat and handing it to her. "I nearly forgot about bringing this."

Inside the box, beneath a swath of tissue paper, she found the white peignoir she'd painted on the lingerie shop window. She glanced up at him. "It's beautiful, Spence, but this van gets pretty cold at night . . ."

"I know. Except it isn't now."

"Except now," she agreed, smiling.

"Put it on for me, so I can see . . ."

She stood and slipped her arms through the sleeves.

"Perfect," he murmured, tying the red satin belt around her waist.

"I shouldn't keep it."

"Yes, you should. I bought it for our wedding night."

"Spence, you've got to stop this. I'm not leaving here with any promises. No matter how much I care for you, I have to settle on a career before I—"

"Dammit, I've tried to be patient, but I'm sick of hearing that! You have a career. You paint windows."

"That's not a career, that's just a job. Surely even you can see the difference."

He stared at her. "*Even* me? What do you mean by that crack?"

"I mean that I don't think you really care whether I settle into satisfying work or not, so long as I stay in your life, in your bed."

"Not true, dammit!"

"You're swearing a lot," she observed coldly.

"Maybe I have to swear to get the point across. I've watched you paint windows and I think you happen to enjoy it very much. The work is flexible, so you can also take on other projects, community service things, for example. You're your own boss. You can be extremely creative. What the hell more do you want?"

"You think I can go around telling people that's what I do for a living? Paint store windows?"

He gazed at her silently. "I don't know why not, but apparently you have some high-flown idea of what makes a job worthwhile."

"Of course I do! I've been told all my life that I'm talented, that I can do anything I want, that I shouldn't waste my abilities. What do you call painting store windows? Is that discovering the cure for cancer, or improving literacy, or even giving people better teeth, for heaven's sake?"

"Maybe not, but—"

"You're just afraid that my search will take me away from you, that's all."

"Maybe I am. In fact, sure I am, but that's not the point. I don't think you see what—"

"I see one thing. You'd better leave. Now."

"You're one stubborn woman, Jill Amory."

"Good! It's about time! All my life I've drifted whichever way the wind blew. Now it's time for *me* to call the shots." She pointed to her chest. "Me."

"Well, you're sure doing that, sweetheart." He opened the door, letting in a blast of cold air that whipped through the filmy peignoir. "See you around," he said, and leaped to the ground.

She closed and locked the door behind him. Pushing the curtain aside, she watched him walk away through swirling snow. When he was out of sight, she realized she was shivering violently. It was very cold in the van.

JILL SLEPT LITTLE that night, but all through the dark hours she told herself that the fight was a good thing. She could leave more easily now that she knew how Spence really felt. He'd be content for her to spend her life in a pursuit no more important than decorating windows. What a laugh. Except that she didn't feel like laughing.

The next morning she drove to a mall across town from the Remembrance to find a wedding present for Charlie and Gladys. Over the weekend, while she'd toured the city, she'd tried to think of an appropriate gift, but her usually creative mind had failed her. Today was her last chance. She wanted to take her gift to the late-night supper in the mall that evening.

Robert had arranged the supper for members of the wedding party so that Gladys's daughter and granddaughter would have a chance to meet Charlie before the ceremony the next morning. Jill felt obligated to attend, although she'd rather have avoided seeing Spence.

Finding the right gift wasn't easy, considering that Gladys had everything she needed, and Jill couldn't imagine what would be appropriate for an old fellow who believed that he was St. Valentine. By noon she'd nearly given up hope that she'd find something, when she passed an art supply store and inspiration hit. Later, with an armload of supplies, she drove back to the Remembrance Mall.

Fortunately the snow had stopped during the night, and today the sky formed a brilliant blue backdrop for the Victorian gingerbread of the mall. Jill set up her easel, unpacked her newly purchased watercolors and began. She discarded several drafts, stopping only to eat a sandwich, before she finished something that she liked. As light faded from the sky, she stood back to admire her work while the colors dried. Luckily her training had turned out to be good for something and she had the perfect memento for Gladys and Charlie.

She knew they'd enjoy the painting, but Jill never had kidded herself that she was good enough for the competitive world of art. Window decorations and an occasional landscape for a friend encompassed her abilities. She'd hardly call that a career, although Spence seemed willing to do so. Ah, well, he just didn't understand that she had to find a career that would make a difference in the world.

She packed her gear back into the van and returned to the campground, where she matted and framed the painting with materials she'd also bought that afternoon. Finding still more time on her hands, she designed a card, congratulating the "King and Queen of Hearts." The supper was to begin at eleven, because Charlie had thought it would be romantic to toast his and Gladys's happiness at midnight.

By ten Jill had wrapped the framed picture in silver striped paper and topped it with an elaborate bow. Then she put the package aside and dressed for the dinner in her jeans and matching vest. She'd decided to save her new suit for the ceremony the next morning, although Gladys had assured her that jeans would be fine for the wedding, too.

"I've told the Senior Striders they can all wear jogging outfits if they want to," Gladys had said. "I considered it myself, until Charlie talked me into that romantic gown I showed you."

Jill was happy for the two of them, although their devotion to each other gave her a bittersweet pang. Love and commitment seemed so far away for her.

At last, carrying her package, she approached the mall entrance designated as the one the party-goers would use. Bernie, without his walking stick and wearing a coat and tie for the first time since she'd met him, was stationed at the glass door to let people in. He smiled and opened the door.

"I'm sure glad you're here," he said. "Maybe you can talk some sense into them."

"Who?"

"Charlie and Gladys. There's some sort of hullabaloo over there, but I've been stuck by the door and I can't tell what's going on."

Jill glanced toward the skating pond, where several linen-draped tables topped with flickering hurricane lamps surrounded the pond. Nearby a long buffet table heaped with food and crowned with a Cupid ice sculpture stood untouched. The guests huddled in two groups, one male with Charlie in the middle, the other female with Gladys in the middle.

"I have a feeling Gladys's daughter has something to do with it," Bernie said. "She's the blonde holding that little girl by the hand. Gladys introduced me when they came through the door. The son-in-law couldn't leave work on such short notice, but the daughter's here, and I don't think she approves of Charlie."

"I can understand how a daughter might be worried," Jill said, "but if she gets to know Charlie, she'll feel better about this."

"I suppose. But I thought of something else. Maybe the daughter's miffed because she wasn't asked to be the matron of honor."

"Oh, dear!" Jill exclaimed, aware for the first time of her awkward position in the wedding party. "Of course she could be. I feel like a dummy for not thinking of that. I'll be glad to step aside, Bernie. You're right. Gladys should have asked her daughter."

"I don't know if your stepping aside would do much good. Then the daughter might feel like second choice."

"You're right. What a mess!"

"I could be mistaken," Bernie said. "Maybe that's not the problem at all."

"There's only one way to find out. Spence isn't here yet?" Jill asked.

"Not yet. He— Oh, here he comes now." Bernie stepped back and opened the door.

Jill turned and met Spence's dark gaze for a moment, but the pain was too fresh from the night before and she glanced away. He'd brought his gift, too, a large package he carried under one arm. "Bernie says the happy couple has a problem," she said, keeping her gaze averted.

Spence unzipped his jacket. "Sounds like par for the course."

Jill winced. His remark, coupled with an action that reminded her of when he'd last unzipped a jacket in her presence, dug into the core of her unhappiness and lodged there like a piece of sharp glass.

"Any idea what the problem is?" Spence asked Bernie.

"Not for sure, but Gladys's daughter has something to do with it, I'll bet. I figured you and Jill might be able to help. She could infiltrate the women's group and you could find out what's going on with the men."

"You're sure they're fighting?" Spence asked, gazing at the two clusters of people.

"I'm sure all right, even from here. The party started out with everyone mixed in together. Gladys and Charlie were holding hands. Then Gladys started talking with that blonde, who's her daughter, and the little girl, who's really up past her bedtime, not that it's my business."

"She looks like she's only about five," Jill commented. "It is pretty late."

"I think she's here because Gladys dotes on her and couldn't bear to have a sitter. Anyway, after discussing something with her daughter, Gladys went back to talk with Charlie, only this time her face looked different, not so happy, and then they had some sharp words with each other. Again I could tell by the faces. After that Gladys ran over to one side, and all the women followed, while Charlie stayed where he was and all the men gathered around him."

"That sounds like a fight," Spence agreed.

"Yep," Bernie agreed. "I really hate to see Gladys looking so miserable. She's . . . a wonderful woman."

Jill glanced at Bernie. Poor guy, he was sweet on Gladys, too, she thought. That was why he'd been watching the proceedings with such concentration.

"I'll bet you two can patch things up," Bernie said, smiling. "You make a good team."

"So they say," Spence commented, glancing at Jill. "Ready to tackle it, teammate?"

"I guess we'd better do something," she said, ignoring the sarcasm in his tone. "We can't have them splitting up the night before their wedding."

"Nope. If that's going to happen, it's better to do it early in the relationship," Spence said, his gaze unyielding. "By the way, Bernie," he said, turning toward the older man, "my folks will be along in a little while. Dad was doing some chores, as usual, and didn't start getting ready on time. I hope they aren't late to the wedding tomorrow."

"I hope there's a wedding they shouldn't be late to," Bernie replied. "You two go over and work a miracle, okay?"

"Sure." Spence took Jill's elbow and guided her toward the two groups of people. "Feel in the miracle-working mood?" he asked softly.

"No."

"I didn't think so. What did you get them for a gift?"

"I spent the afternoon painting a watercolor of the mall and framing it."

Spence chuckled. "You're kidding."

Stung by his reaction, she jerked her elbow from his grasp. "I'm sorry if you think that's a dopey idea. I don't."

"I don't think it's a dopey idea. I couldn't come up with anything, and finally this afternoon I asked Mom and

Dad if we could give them the architect's first scale model of this place. They said fine. It's packed in this box." He glanced at her. "Interesting coincidence."

"Mmm."

"Charlie and Gladys don't look very happy," Spence commented.

"No, they don't."

"Okay, here's the plan. You find out Gladys's complaints, and I'll get Charlie's side of the story. Then maybe the four of us can take a walk around the mall, away from all these people, and work something out."

"Just walking or race-walking?"

He smiled faintly. "I'm glad you've still got your sense of humor. Okay, teammate, go get 'em." He squeezed her arm and headed for the group of men.

Tears pricked her eyes at his unexpected touch and affectionate encouragement. If only... But Spence wanted to limit her horizons, she reminded herself. With a sigh she walked over to the women.

Gladys greeted her with subdued courtesy and introduced her daughter Ginny and granddaughter Beth. Stephanie from Jegger Outfitters was there, and Hedda Kramer, and several female members of the Senior Striders. During the introductions, Ginny displayed no hostility toward Jill. Perhaps Bernie had been wrong about her, Jill thought. Still, she had to approach the discussion with tact, in case she was inadvertently part of the problem.

"I'm amazed that you all haven't started in on that delicious buffet," she said.

Gladys twisted her engagement ring, which Jill knew she'd paid for herself. "You might as well know that Charlie and I are having a little, um, altercation," she said quietly.

"I suspected you might be," Jill said, dropping any pretense that she hadn't noticed the divided camps. She glanced at Ginny. "I hope none of it has to do with me."

"With you?" Gladys looked confused. "Why would it have to do with you?"

"Well, I wondered if your daughter might be upset because Charlie asked me to be the maid of honor." Jill thought putting the finger on Charlie, where it in truth belonged, might help.

"That bothered me at first," Ginny admitted, "but after talking with Charlie earlier today I realized the poor man hadn't meant to hurt anybody by asking you first. He was so apologetic that I couldn't be angry with him. No, I'm afraid the problem's more lasting than that."

"And it's all my fault," Gladys said. "I should have listened to Charlie more carefully, but I was so in love, that I . . ."

"I understand," Jill said, patting her shoulder. Boy, did she understand.

"I guess the idea of traveling around all the time never really sank in," Gladys continued. "Charlie told me there would be lots of traveling, but I didn't realize we'd have no home base at all until Ginny wondered how often we'd be coming back to Colorado. I asked Charlie, and he said he didn't know. Maybe every couple of years, he said, or maybe longer, depending on . . . his business."

Jill could tell from Gladys's hesitation that she hadn't confided to Ginny that Charlie believed he was St. Valentine. Jill glanced at Ginny's no-nonsense hairstyle and tailored clothes and agreed with Gladys's decision. "I suppose you'd have to sell your town house," Jill commented.

Gladys nodded. "That's not what really bothers me, though. I'm afraid I'd never see Ginny or Beth. And without a fixed address, they couldn't visit me, either. Then there are my friends, especially these gals, who've been in the Senior Striders with me. I...suppose I'm more settled in Colorado than I thought." She gazed over at Charlie, who was deep in conversation with Spence. "But I really love him," she added softly. "In spite of it all."

Gladys's last statement echoed exactly what Jill had been thinking about Spence. So why did these men have to cause such problems? How dared Charlie allow this crazy fantasy of his to jeopardize the happiness of such a wonderful woman? "I think we need to talk to Charlie," she said, her lips set in a grim line as she took Gladys's arm. "If you all will excuse us, we'll be back in a little while. In the meantime, why doesn't everyone enjoy the buffet?"

"Want me to come along, Mom?" Ginny asked.

"That's okay, dear," Gladys said with a wavering smile. "Jill knows all the, uh, background. I haven't had a chance to fill you in on everything, but later we'll talk."

Ginny looked doubtful. "All right. And good luck."

"Thanks." A few steps away, Gladys whispered in Jill's ear. "I haven't told her about St. Valentine."

"I didn't suppose you had."

"I remember how you reacted, and Ginny's even more matter-of-fact than you are."

The statement surprised her with its implication that she was matter-of-fact. Jill of All Trades, who followed her every whim? Yet Gladys didn't perceive her that way at all.

Spence must have seen their approach from the corner of his eye, because he steered Charlie away from the group and toward Jill and Gladys. "Anyone for a walk?"

he called out as they drew close to each other. "I've heard this is a terrific place for it."

"I don't have on the right outfit," Gladys said, glancing down at her long gown and high heels.

"We'll take it easy," Jill assured her.

"Maybe for once I can keep up with you, Gladys, my dear," Charlie said with a sad smile.

"Oh, Charlie," Gladys said, gazing at him with suspiciously bright eyes.

"Let's go," Spence urged, starting them off at a gentle pace.

They assembled themselves four abreast, with Spence on the left end, Charlie next, Jill next to him, and Gladys on the right.

Jill turned to Charlie. "I don't care what Spence or the other men told you, but you have to give up this St. Valentine stuff. You've offered your hand to a fine woman and now you want to tear her away from her family to live like some gypsy because of this wild fantasy of yours. For her sake, and for yours, you must—"

"That's precisely what Spencer told me," Charlie said, interrupting her tirade.

"He did?" Jill glanced over at Spence in admiration and love.

"Of course I did," Spence said, gazing at her as they walked slowly down the deserted mall. "That shouldn't surprise you, that I'd advise someone to go for the love instead of the career."

She swallowed. "Sometimes it doesn't have to be a choice."

"That's true, but when it does . . ."

"You're both absolutely right," Charlie said in the ensuing silence. "That's why I'm retiring as St. Valentine and staying here with Gladys. They'll simply have to find a replacement for me."

"Charlie, that's wonderful!" Jill stopped and grabbed him in a bear hug. "Gladys, isn't that super?" she asked, turning to the gray-haired woman. "Now you can have everything you wanted . . . Gladys, what's the matter?"

"I thought that was what I wanted, but . . . I can't let him do that," Gladys said, her voice quavering. "His work is too important."

Jill was stunned. "His work?" she asked faintly. "But, Gladys, you don't really think, deep down in your heart, that Charlie . . ."

"Yes, I really do." Gladys took Jill's hand and reached for Spence's. Gently she placed their hands together. "Look at what has happened with the two of you because of Charlie. You're so much in love that it's wonderful to watch."

Jill stood speechless as Spence held her hand and gazed into her eyes.

"When Charlie told me he wanted to have our wedding on February fourteenth and ask both of you to be there because that would guarantee your own marriage, I agreed immediately," Gladys continued. "I thought about my daughter being matron of honor, but I decided to help Charlie work this magic for the two of you instead. My daughter had found her true love, but you were still uncertain whether you had, and I knew how much you deserved each other."

Jill shook her head to clear it. "This is crazy," she said, taking her hand from Spence's. Somebody had to inject a note of sanity around here. "Spence and I had a rather large disagreement of our own last night, and I doubt that we'll be seeing each other again after tomorrow. So, Gladys, please don't sacrifice your happiness so that

Charlie can continue with his work. I'm afraid it's a fantasy. A lovely fantasy, to be sure, but still not one worth calling off this marriage for."

"In that case, my dear," Charlie said, "I certainly must retire. If I've failed with you and Spencer, that proves that the job belongs to a younger, more vigorous man."

Jill's heart ached to hear his despairing words, but wasn't this all for the best?

"Nonsense!" Gladys walked over to Charlie and stood before him like a commanding general. "Unless you continue with your work, Charlie Hartman, I will never speak to you again. That's a promise."

"But, Gladys . . ."

"And as for you, young lady," Gladys said, turning toward Jill, "you have the arrogance of youth. Perhaps when you're my age, you'll have the good sense to believe in magic. Or perhaps—" She consulted her watch. "Perhaps now that it's one minute past twelve, you'll begin to believe a little sooner than that." She gazed triumphantly at Charlie. "You see? It's February fourteenth, and these two are face-to-face, as we planned."

"So they are," Charlie said, "but what if my powers have, indeed, faded? You heard Jill. They had a tremendous disagreement last evening."

"What about?" Gladys demanded, looking at Spence. He shook his head. "Better talk to Jill about that."

Gladys folded her arms and faced Jill. "Well? We told you all our problems, so don't be shy about telling us yours."

Jill fidgeted under Gladys's scrutiny. Finally she squared her shoulders and lifted her chin. "All my life I've been told I could do anything I wanted, because I have talents. But talents carry responsibilities, right? Charlie would have to agree with that."

"I do," Charlie replied.

"So I'm struggling to find something worthwhile to do with my life. Spence told me he thought painting window decorations was just fine, and to forget my high-flown ambitions to make a difference in the world."

"I did not! I merely said that—"

"Stop this," Gladys said, holding up her hand. "Honestly, I'd forgotten how young people fight, without ever stopping to listen. Now, Jill, I'm going to tell you something I've learned. You may have to think about it for a while, but please think about it. Will you do that?"

"Of course. I spend lots of time thinking."

"And she has to think alone," Spence added with a trace of mockery.

"Spence, that's enough!" Gladys said, pointing a finger in his direction. "You don't understand this woman's dilemma, and you're riding roughshod over her feelings."

"But I—"

"Enough, I said. Now, Jill, everyone meant well when they told you that you could do anything you wanted, because you're talented. But they unknowingly put a burden on you, too. You think you have to become something great for them. What you become must be for yourself, not others."

"But—"

"Just a minute. You're not allowed to interrupt me any more than Spencer is. Now listen. This is important. If you do what makes you happy, you'll fulfill all your potential. Think about that. Does painting windows make you happy?"

"Yes, but—"

"Then paint windows. Does helping with a community project, like this mall thing, make you happy?"

"Yes, but—"

"Then do that. Jill, you are perfectly fine as you are. Believe me, you will make a difference in the world. The world doesn't have many people in it who are truly happy. Be one of them, and you'll change lives."

Jill stared at her.

"You don't think I'm right, do you?"

She shook her head.

Gladys shrugged. "It takes time."

Charlie stepped forward and took Gladys's hands in his. "I know now why I fell in love with you, dear lady. Isn't there some way we can resolve this conundrum between us?"

Gladys's military stance softened. "No," she said softly. "As much as these two belong together as husband and wife, we don't. You must continue your vagabond life-style to be truly happy, and I must stay close to my family and friends. I . . . wasn't thinking clearly before."

"I will give it all up for you, you know," Charlie said.

"I know, and I love you for it, but I couldn't live with myself if I tied you down like that."

"May I . . . may I visit you now and then?"

"You don't even have to ask that, dear man. Now perhaps we'd better go back and inform the guests that there's been a change in plans."

"Yes, my dear, I suppose we must." Charlie offered his arm and Gladys took it. It seemed as if they'd forgotten Jill and Spence existed as they smiled at each other and began walking down the mall.

Jill watched them with tears in her eyes. How could they agree so bravely to live apart? Surely it was because they were both a little crazy. Normal people would cling to each other and never let go, but not these two.

Spence moved up beside her. "Well, Miss Jill Amory? What now?"

"It's ridiculous," Jill said around the lump in her throat. "I can't believe they're acting this way."

"Oh, I don't know. What Gladys said a while ago made some sense to me."

"I think you'd be foolish to believe anything she said, or Charlie, either, for that matter," Jill said, angry with both of them for deciding to part.

"So you don't buy this stuff about doing what makes you happy, and fulfilling your obligation to the world that way?"

"It's romantic claptrap, just like everything else they say."

"They won't be getting married tomorrow," he said quietly. "I guess you're free to leave."

She turned slowly and faced him. "Yes, I guess I am."

14

JILL ARRIVED in Bangor, Maine, on the tenth of June, two days before her birthday. She'd phoned her mother and G.G. the night before to let them know she was coming. Her apartment wouldn't be vacant until the first of July, so she'd asked to stay in her old room at home until then.

G.G. was waiting for her on the porch of the shingled two-story house where Jill had grown up. G.G.'s progress down the cement stairs was unsteady, but her face glowed with delight as Jill pulled into the drive, windows rolled down to catch the cool Maine air. "She's here, Nelda!" G.G. called over her shoulder. "Our Jill is here!"

Our Jill. She remembered how Charlie used to call her that. Colorado seemed so far away. Colorado and all that had happened there with Charlie, Gladys, Tippy the Lip, Bernie, George, Robert and, of course, Spence Jegger. She'd expected to miss him; she hadn't expected to feel as if her heart had been ripped out and replaced with a chunk of lead.

Seeing G.G.'s smiling face helped. Jill hopped out of the van and hurried over to hug her beloved great-grandmother and breathe in the familiar violet scent of her cologne. "Did you get my last postcard?"

"It's already pasted in the scrapbook, my dear!" G.G. exclaimed, smiling at her. "Come along, let me take a peek at that map on your van. I've been waiting a year to see all those states colored in. My, will you look at that."

Jill had forgotten that G.G. also used the expression "my dear," as Charlie had. No wonder Charlie had seemed like an old friend from the start.

"Jill, sweetheart!"

Jill turned as her mother ran down the steps, her salt-and-pepper hair bouncing, her smile wide. Jill hugged her with enthusiasm. She'd missed these two and she was touched at how much they seemed to have missed her.

"Let me look at you," her mother said, holding out Jill's hands and studying her from head to toe. "You've let your hair grow longer. I suppose that saved on expenses, not to have it cut. I'll treat you to a beauty salon visit this week."

"Thanks, Mom, but I think I'll skip the haircut," Jill said.

"Oh? I thought you never liked having it too long."

"I think *you* never liked having it too long," Jill said with a teasing smile.

"Grown independent now that you've been out on your own, have you?"

"Yes."

"Well, unload your things and come inside. I have to check on supper," her mother said, climbing the steps to the porch. "Oh, and Aaron's been pestering us every day to find out when you'd be here, so you'd better call him right away."

"Don't forget that other fellow who's been calling," G.G. said. "What was his name, Nelda?"

"Let me think," Jill's mother said, pausing as she opened the screen door. "Was it Chad? No...sorry, I can't remember." She went into the house.

Jill's heart pounded. "Was his first name Spence?" she asked her great-grandmother.

"No, that wasn't it," G.G. said. "Charlie, I think. Charlie Harmon, or something like that."

"Charlie Hartman," Jill said, as disappointment flooded her. During the whole drive today she'd wondered if she'd come home to a message from Spence. This was the only place he could have tracked her down since she'd left Colorado Springs. Instead Charlie was still acting as the perennial matchmaker, although she was surprised he'd call long distance when he had so little money.

"That's it," G.G. said. "Charlie Hartman. He mentioned some business deal you two had, and he wanted to follow up. He sounded like an older fellow. Did you paint some store windows for him?"

"No," Jill said with a sad smile as she stepped into the van and came back with an armload of her possessions. "He, um, tried to interest me in another venture, but it didn't work out."

"Who's Spence?"

Jill glanced away from G.G.'s bright eyes. "Oh, someone I met."

"Just someone you met, huh? I don't think so."

"Anyway, it doesn't matter." Jill started toward the house at a pace slow enough for G.G. "I've finished my trip, but I still haven't found a career to follow. From that standpoint, I still feel like a failure."

"If that isn't rubbish, I don't know what is," G.G. said, tottering along beside her. "You're not a failure. You have the whole world before you. You can do anything you set your mind to."

Jill paused and looked down at her great-grandmother. "Have you ever thought," she said slowly, surprising herself by her statement, "that being able to do 'anything I set my mind to' could make my decision even harder?"

G.G. leaned on her cane. "Can't say I have. I figured you were the lucky one, having so many interests and abilities."

"But the implication's always been that I'll accomplish something really great, once I 'set my mind to it.'"

"And I believe you will." G.G. gazed at her with pride.

Jill's stomach tightened in the old, familiar way. Had Gladys been right, after all? Jill started toward the house again. "Maybe," she said.

The living room smelled of lemon oil and the aroma of baked chicken drifted from the kitchen. Nelda Amory was an excellent cook and a zealous housekeeper. Her motto had always been "If a job's worth doing, it's worth doing right." Jill thought of that motto as she kissed G.G. on the cheek and started up the stairs to the bedroom that had been hers until she'd moved into an apartment six years ago.

Her mother hadn't changed her room. The framed certificates for high grades, the ribbons for art shows, her high school graduation tassel, still hung on the walls. To that display she'd added posters, all of which had a similar theme—*Climb Every Mountain*, *Dream the Impossible Dream*, *Reach for the Stars*. Nothing about this room advised her to find the path that made her happy, only the road that led to glory.

She might have left this room six years ago, she thought, but she'd taken its messages with her. The weight of those messages had lifted some during the past year, because she'd convinced herself that somewhere along the way she'd have a revelation and know what to do with her life. It hadn't happened.

As she placed her bundle of clothes and her purse on the bed, the telephone on the bedside table rang. She didn't answer. She wasn't quite up to Aaron at the moment.

"Jill!" her mother called up the stairs. "It's that Charlie Harmon fellow."

Jill reached for the receiver immediately. Charlie didn't have long-distance money to spare, and besides, he was a link with Spence. "Charlie?" she said warmly. "How are you?"

"I'm fine, my dear. I was wondering if I might see you."

"See me? Aren't you in Colorado?"

"I'm in Bangor, Maine," Charlie said.

"Here? How did you get here? Are you alone?" Her first wild thought was that Spence and Charlie had traveled to Maine together.

"Yes, I'm alone," Charlie replied, dashing her hopes. "Could we have a little chat this evening, perhaps?"

"Why, of course. Where are you staying? Would you like to come over for supper?"

"That would be lovely, but I hesitate to inconvenience your mother."

"I'm sure she's cooked enough to feed half the town. Tell me where you are and I'll come and pick you up. If I remember Mom's usual schedule, she'll be serving dinner in about half an hour." Jill wondered if he needed a place to stay, but she decided to deal with that later.

"I really won't need a lift, my dear. I'll find my way to your house. Everyone seems quite friendly here."

"They are, but I insist on picking you up. Just—"

"I'll be there shortly," Charlie interrupted, and hung up.

Jill frowned and replaced the receiver. Charlie probably had no place to stay and didn't want her to find out.

She'd have to work on him after dinner. At least for the time he was in Bangor, she'd make sure he had a roof over his head. In a way, she wished that Gladys had agreed to travel with him; she could have paid for hotel rooms. But that wouldn't have been the best life for Gladys, in the long run, and people needed to do what was best for themselves. My, that sounded selfish, Jill thought, glancing up at her posters. Then she hurried downstairs to tell her mother there would be a guest for dinner.

CHARLIE WON HER MOTHER'S and G.G.'s hearts with his courtly ways, as Jill had expected he would. He glossed over his travel arrangements and referred vaguely to "my hotel" without giving a name, giving the impression of an eccentric old man using his retirement checks to travel the globe. Jill was convinced he was sleeping on a park bench somewhere, unless Spence had managed to force money on him for the trip to Maine.

Charlie regaled them with the story of Tippy the Lip's attempt to ruin the Remembrance Mall, and he made Jill sound like Joan of Arc as he recounted her part in the fight to save the trolley and the museum. Mercifully for Jill, he kept Spence's name out of the narration. Jill knew G.G. would pick up on it and make the connection.

"So I had to stop in and see that map after it was finished," Charlie said, patting his mouth with one of the linen napkins Jill's mother had set out for the occasion.

"Jill is an amazing girl, that's for sure," G.G. said, beaming. "Why, she could do anything, anything at all."

Charlie glanced at Jill. "She's very clever with those window decorations, you know."

"It was a wonderful way to earn her travel money," her mother agreed. "Window decoration is hardly what I'd call a career, but it served the purpose."

"What would you call a career, Mrs. Amory?" Charlie put his napkin beside his plate and leaned back in his chair.

Jill noticed that the button of his vest strained a little across his stomach and she smiled. At least he'd had one good meal in Bangor.

"Why, a career means doing something significant," Jill's mother replied.

"Have you had one, would you say?"

"Mercy, no. I haven't done anything to brag about."

"Except keep a beautiful home and cook marvelous meals and raise an exceptional daughter," Charlie said.

Nelda Amory blushed. "That's hardly a career, Mr. Hartman."

"Have you been happy?"

"Well, yes. I've missed having my husband these past ten years, of course, but otherwise, yes. I've been lucky that he left me very well provided for."

"I'll wager you also do a share of volunteer work in the community," Charlie said.

"She certainly does," G.G. confirmed. "Why, some of the local charities wouldn't manage without her."

"And you do your part, too, Grandmother Amory," Nelda said, blushing even more. "You're all making me out to be some sort of person I'm not. Especially compared to people who really make a difference, like Jill's Aaron, for example."

Jill winced. He wasn't "her Aaron" at all, and she didn't want Charlie to get that idea and relay it to Spence. But she couldn't think what to say without causing a stir, so she remained silent.

"Aaron has developed some wonderful new techniques for gold crowns," Jill's mother continued. "That's so important for people, to have good teeth, or at least good substitute teeth, don't you think, Mr. Hartman? Aaron performs a real service for the community as a dentist."

"Well, yes, I suppose," Charlie said.

Jill could hold back no longer. "Mom, I hate to burst your bubble, but Aaron told me before he even went to dental school that he was in it for the money. He specializes in gold crowns because that's an expensive procedure and brings in more money."

Nelda Amory's eyes widened. "Of course he makes a good living. There's nothing wrong with that, but in the meantime, he has a worthwhile career that—"

"In the meantime he's a very unhappy man," Jill interrupted. "What he really wanted to do was raise cocker spaniels, but his parents made such fun of that idea he finally chose dental school. He may not have the nerve until after his parents die, but I'll bet eventually he'll give up dentistry to raise dogs."

"That's crazy," muttered Jill's mother. "All that training would be down the drain."

"And he's so smart," G.G. added. "He was another one, like Jill, who could have done anything he wanted. Why would he want to raise little dogs?"

"Maybe because he loves little dogs," Jill said. She glanced at Charlie and absorbed his approving smile. Joy bubbled up in her; the revelation she'd traveled all over the country to find had finally burst upon her. The year she'd spent painting holiday windows she'd been happy, happier than ever before. Getting the orders, dreaming up clever pictures and messages, and finally viewing the results of her imagination had been fun. Along the way she'd found chances to be of service to people, and she'd wanted to help them because the happiness she'd found in her work promoted a desire to help other people find happiness, too. At last it all made sense.

"Dessert, Mr. Hartman?" Jill's mother asked, rising to clear the plates.

"You're too kind," Charlie said, "but I'm afraid I'm completely satiated. Perhaps if Jill and I might sit on your front porch swing for a bit, I could manage some of what I'm certain is a mouth-watering treat."

"I'll be right there, Charlie, after I help with the dishes," Jill said.

"In that case, perhaps I, too, should help," Charlie said, pushing back his chair. "Forgive me for not offering in the first place."

"Heavens, no," Jill's mother said, waving them toward the living room. "You're our guest and this is Jill's first night home in a year. Both of you go out and enjoy the night air."

Charlie looked doubtful and glanced at Jill.

"You might as well not argue with Mom on an issue like this," Jill said, chuckling. "Thanks, Mom. I'll make it up to you."

"I'm sure you will, sweetheart. You always were a good helper," her mother said. "Now you two go and have a talk. I imagine you'd like to catch up on each other's news."

Moments later Jill and Charlie swayed gently in the old porch swing and watched an occasional car drive by on the residential street. Jill wanted to ask about Spence, but didn't know where to begin, so she sat waiting for Charlie to open the conversation.

"Aren't you curious about him?" Charlie asked finally.

There was no need for Jill to ask who Charlie meant. They both knew. "Yes, of course . . ."

"Spencer is what you modern people would call a basket case," Charlie said. "It's a wonder the store is functioning at all. If he hadn't trained Stephanie and Horace so well, it might not be."

"Oh, dear." Jill's heart hammered. Did he really love her that much?

"I couldn't do very much for the poor boy until you arrived in Maine, but about two weeks ago I decided to set out for Bangor and discover how you had fared on your journey."

"How did you get here?"

"That's not important," Charlie said. "I believe I've seen what I hoped to see. Am I correct?"

She turned to him. "Charlie, can I really go back to Colorado Springs and do nothing more worthwhile than paint holiday windows?"

"No, you can't."

"What? But I saw you smile when I mentioned Aaron's dogs, and—"

"Let me explain, my dear. You will never 'just paint windows.' Service to others is in your blood, and you can no more ignore the urge to help people than fly. So you will paint windows, and do all the other wonderful helpful things for which you were born. Perhaps someday you'll tire of painting windows and start another business. It doesn't matter. Follow your heart, and you'll be fine."

"If I follow my heart, I'll leave for Colorado in the morning."

"Excellent." Charlie took out his handkerchief and polished his gold lapel pin. "That's what I traveled all this way to hear."

Jill laughed, feeling giddy with happiness. "I suppose you'll take the credit, too, for making sure Spence and I were together on St. Valentine's Day."

"Would you deny me that small satisfaction?"

"Absolutely not, Charlie." She leaned over and kissed his lined cheek. "Thank you, St. Valentine."

"Goodness, you'll have me blushing!"

"Red is your color," she teased.

"That it is. So you will leave in the morning, early?"

"I feel like taking off right now, but unfortunately I have to talk with Aaron before I go and tell him that we're finished. Besides, if I left tonight, right after I got here, Mom and G.G. would be upset. I have to explain everything to them first, and sleep, if I possibly can. Spence and I will fly Mom and G.G. out for the wedding, of course, and Charlie, you simply have to be Spence's best man."

"That sounds like quite an honor, my dear."

"Why don't you ride back to Colorado with me? In fact, I was going to ask you to stay here overnight, anyway. Don't tell me that you already have a hotel room, because I know better."

Charlie smiled. "You see? You're bound and determined to assist others."

"So you'll stay?"

"Let me think about it. In the meantime, why don't you let your mother know that I'd be delighted to sample her dessert?"

"Oh, you will be delighted, Charlie," she said, leaving the swing. "She makes the best carrot cake in town."

"Sounds marvelous."

Jill hurried inside to the kitchen, where she announced that she and Charlie were ready for dessert. "And, Mom, I'm not convinced that Charlie has a place to stay the night," she added, deciding to save her big news for later. "Could he use the guest room, just for tonight?"

"Certainly, sweetheart," her mother said. "He's a nice old man and I'd be glad to have him."

"Thanks, Mom." Jill gave her a hug and then gave G.G. a hug, too. "You've been a wonderful influence on me, both of you," she said, and meant it. Their desire to see her settled in a prestigious career was understandable. And because they loved her, they'd learn to accept her plans, whatever they were.

She returned to the porch in high spirits. "Charlie, they're dishing the—" She stopped and glanced quickly around the empty porch. Then she ran down the steps and looked up and down the deserted street. He was gone.

JILL TIMED HER RETURN to the Remembrance Mall to coincide with closing time. She couldn't resist the drama of a surprise entrance. Charlie might have already given her away, though. She'd spent two solid hours the morning before she left Bangor looking for him on every park bench. She'd called all the hotels and motels. Finally she'd accepted that he didn't want to be found and would make his own way back. Disappointed, but anxious to be on her way, she'd kissed her mother and G.G. goodbye and pointed the van toward Colorado.

She walked into the mall at five minutes before nine. Her heart was pounding as she approached Jegger Outfitters. He could be out in front, but she hoped that he was back in the storeroom, where she could greet him in private.

The front of the store was empty except for Stephanie, who was totaling out the cash register. When Jill walked in, Stephanie opened her mouth to call out a de-lighted greeting, but Jill put her finger to her lips.

"He's in the back," Stephanie said, her eyes dancing. "And am I glad to see you. He's been a bear to work for for the past few months."

"I'm sorry," Jill apologized. "I had to iron some things out."

"That happens," Stephanie said. "Now go on back there. He's bought a new chess set and is playing with an imaginary partner."

"Charlie's not here?"

"Charlie? Haven't seen him for about three weeks."

"Oh. I thought . . . Oh, well. Wish me luck."

"Trust me, you won't need it," Stephanie said with a chuckle as Jill walked toward the storeroom.

Jill wasn't sure her legs would hold her as she drew back the curtain and stepped into the semidarkness of the storeroom. In this very spot they'd shared their first kiss. Longing rushed over her as she started toward the light where Charlie's little apartment had been.

"I'll be there in a minute, Steph," Jill heard him say as she approached. Apparently he'd heard her footsteps and thought she was Stephanie. "I've almost—" He looked up as Jill walked through the makeshift doorway.

The expression on his face would stay with her al-ways. With a cry she ran into his arms, and tears coursed down her cheeks as he kissed her over and over.

"Jill, oh, my Jill," he murmured, touching her face, her hands, gazing into her eyes. "I prayed that's what Char-lie's letter meant, that you were coming back, but I was afraid to let myself believe it completely."

"I love you," she said, pronouncing each word with firm emphasis.

He gazed at her without speaking, and his eyes glistened with moisture. "I wish it hadn't taken you quite so long to find out," he said, his voice thick with emotion.

"So do I. Oh, Spence, so do I."

He cupped her face in both hands. "What happened? What made you decide to come back?"

"A combination of things. When I got home and heard my family talking about my 'doing anything I set my mind to,' I remembered what Gladys had said. I *did* feel the burden of having to choose some wonderful occupation, to fulfill their dreams for me."

"Just having you here fulfills all my dreams." He gazed into her eyes. "Boy, did these four months without you teach me patience. I'm a changed man in that department."

Jill laughed. "That's not the way Stephanie described you a minute ago."

"No? And I thought I was doing so well. Lord, it was tough. No matter how many times Charlie told me the St. Valentine's Day magic would work, I still—"

"Charlie," she said, remembering Spence had mentioned Charlie earlier. "You said something about a letter. Where is he?"

"I don't know."

"You don't? But . . ."

"He left about three weeks ago. Wouldn't take your picture or the model of the mall, as you see." Spence gestured toward Jill's painting hanging on the wall and the scale model perched on the small refrigerator. "I assumed he'd be back. He sent a letter that came today. On the flap it said 'Open when Jill arrives.' It was postmarked in Bangor, so I figured he'd seen you."

"He did, and he helped me sort out some of my feelings, too. Then he disappeared."

"He'll show up," Spence said. "He couldn't resist seeing us together, after all his hard work."

"I hope so. I asked him to be your best man at the wedding. I hope that's all right."

"Mmm." He held her tight. "That's more than all right. Let's talk about the wedding. How soon can we have it?"

"My mother and G.G. will want to be here."

"Didn't you bring them in the van?"

Jill smiled. "That would have been pretty presumptuous. I didn't know for sure if you still wanted me."

He trailed his hand down her throat to the buttons on her blouse. "I think that's my cue. I'd love to prove to you how much I—"

"Spence?" called Stephanie from the front of the store. "Sorry to bother you, but I'm ready to close up."

"Be right there." He grinned self-consciously at Jill. "See what you do to me? I forgot she was here. I might as well let her go home so we can get on with . . . your homecoming celebration."

"Sounds like a wonderful idea."

"You can read Charlie's letter while I'm gone," he said, releasing her and picking up an unopened envelope lying beside the chess set.

"Okay." Jill sat in the chair, still warm from Spence's body, and tore open Charlie's letter. Inside was a folded paper and a small tissue-wrapped package. She examined the letter first. Charlie's gold-embossed stationery featured a crowned letter A, with a Latin inscription beneath it. *"Amor vincit omnia,"* Jill murmured, struggling to remember her high school Latin. "Love . . . conquers . . . all. Love conquers all." Charlie really put his heart into this St. Valentine's business, she thought. Quickly she scanned his message.

Dear Ones,

If you are reading this, then you must be in each other's arms planning a wonderful life together. Alas, but I will not be seeing either of you again. Duty calls. Spencer and Jill, I know you will enjoy every happiness, for you are blessed with the magic of St. Valentine's Day.

Please give my love to Gladys, and convey to her as gently as you can that I won't be seeing her again, either. At one time I selfishly imagined that I might drop by on occasion, but now I realize how inappropriate that would be. Gladys deserves to find a true love who will cherish her as I was unable to do. Bernie is a very likely candidate, and my threatened reappearance might interfere with that. I will miss my friends in the Senior Striders, but truthfully, I won't miss those agonizing race-walks.

My fondest regards,
St. Valentine (Charlie Hartman)

Jill stared at the letter while logic warred with a growing belief that Charlie might be who he claimed to be.

"What did he say?" Spence asked, coming back into the small apartment.

Jill handed him the letter.

"I'll be damned," Spence murmured after reading Charlie's flowing script. "That's it, then?"

"This was in the envelope, too," Jill said, opening the little package in her hand. When the tissue was removed, she held the gold figure-eight pin Charlie had worn on his lapel.

"His infinity pin, that stands for everlasting love," Spence said, hunkering down and gazing at the small object. "He told me he gave that pin away every time he brought a couple together. I asked him where he got new ones, and he said they were sent to him. From where, do you suppose?"

"I can't imagine. This is all too much for me, Spence. You don't suppose that he really. . . ? No, that's crazy."

"Is it?" Spence took the pin and fastened it carefully to Jill's blouse. "Or are we the crazy ones to doubt an old man like Charlie?"

Jill wound her arms around Spence's neck. "At this moment, I don't doubt anything."

"Neither do I, my sweet valentine lady," he murmured, standing up and drawing her into his arms.

"I'll miss Charlie, though." She curved her body against him.

"Me too. But I know we don't need him anymore." He gazed into her eyes. "From now on, we'll make our own magic."

Epilogue

By CONTACTING a few friends, Charlie kept track of Jill's progress from Maine to Colorado Springs, so he had a fair idea when she'd arrive in the Remembrance Mall parking lot. He stationed himself across the street at a bus stop. From there he had a perfect view of the spot where Jill normally parked her van.

His tweed sportcoat provided just enough protection from the June night air. Colorado Springs would be a wonderful place to summer, he thought, if not for the danger of encountering his friends from the Remembrance Mall. No, he couldn't stay, not with Gladys an ever-present temptation to forget his duty.

At fifteen minutes before nine he spied Jill's van pulling into the lot. She parked quickly and hurried toward the mall entrance. Charlie smiled, anticipating the reunion between his two charges. They would accomplish wonderful things during their shared lifetime. Charlie savored the satisfaction of a job well done.

Taking no chances, he stayed at his post until finally, well over two hours later, Jill and Spence emerged, arms around each other's waists, and walked to Spence's black Trans-Am. Charlie stayed in the shadows, although he really didn't fear being seen. The lovers wouldn't have noticed a parade of purple llamas prancing down the street, he thought with a chuckle.

After the black car drove away, Charlie looked around for transportation. While he'd waited for Jill he'd counted a number of eighteen-wheelers going past, but now the street was almost deserted. At last a truck appeared several blocks away, and Charlie stuck out his thumb. As the truck neared, Charlie wrinkled his nose. Livestock. Ah, well, he thought as the driver pulled over and motioned him to get in, beggars couldn't be choosers.

"Where to, buddy?" the trucker asked, eyeing Charlie's mode of dress and his leather briefcase.

"Actually, it doesn't matter," Charlie replied, settling into the roomy seat.

"Well, in any case, I'm headed east," the driver said. "Taking these steers to market."

"I guessed as much." Charlie was already growing accustomed to the odor. "Well, my good man, east is fine with me. My destination is no longer circumscribed by climate."

"Why's that?" the trucker asked.

"I've discovered shopping malls," Charlie said with a smile.

HARLEQUIN *Temptation*

COMING NEXT MONTH

#289 A NEWSWORTHY AFFAIR
Delayne Camp

Asher Ames had done it to her again! And this time, he'd
not only taken a job Tess wanted, he'd be competing with
her every day for entertainment news, too. *He* didn't seem
to think that should stand in the way of their having a torrid
affair, but Tess had a real scoop for *him*.

#290 BOUND FOR BLISS Kristine Rolofson

Henry Myles III was horrified to discover that protecting
his grandfather from a fortune hunter would involve
driving across the country in a twenty-year-old station
wagon with two children, a canary, several smelly land
crabs and the temptress herself, Jess Whalen. Jess was none
too happy about the situation, either. She had no idea what
Henry held against her, but with him in the front seat, it
was going to be a long, long trip....

#291 ANOTHER RAINBOW Lynda Trent

When Rainie Sheenan stumbled upon a hermit in the
mountains above her Tennessee horse farm, she figured it
was her lucky day. Lucas Dalton was gorgeous,
available... and about as far from her citified ex-husband
as she could get. In fact, he was closer in temperament to
her stallion India. But she'd gentled the horse, and she was
determined to tame the man, too.

#292 LOVE NEST Eugenia Riley

When the famous ornithologist Roger Benedict asked
Valerie Vernon to photograph warblers for his latest book,
Valerie knew it was the big career break she'd been waiting
for. But once in the forest, alone with Roger, Valerie
couldn't think of birds without thinking of bees....

Books by Vicki Lewis Thompson

HARLEQUIN TEMPTATION

HARLEQUIN SUPERROMANCE

Don't miss any of our special offers. Write to us at the following address for information on our newest releases.

Harlequin Reader Service
901 Fuhrmann Blvd., P.O. Box 1397, Buffalo, NY 14240
Canadian address: P.O. Box 603,
Fort Erie, Ont. L2A 5X3

The Pirate
JAYNE ANN KRENTZ

At the heart of every powerful romance story lies a legend. There are many romantic legends and countless modern variations on them, but they all have one thing in common: They are tales of brave, resourceful women who must gentle and tame the powerful, passionate men who are their true mates.

The enormous appeal of Jayne Ann Krentz lies in her ability to create modern-day versions of these classic romantic myths, and her LADIES AND LEGENDS trilogy showcases this talent. Believing that a storyteller who can bring legends to life deserves special attention, Harlequin has chosen the first book of the trilogy—THE PIRATE—to receive our Award of Excellence. Look for it now.

AE-PIR-1A

Dear Reader

Thank you for choosing *Forgo[...]*
the world of Lisa and David, the book's two main
characters. To go into any detail about them now
would risk spoiling the story for you, but I can tell
you that they both came to mean a great deal to me
as I took the journey with them and I'm hopeful they
will have the same effect on you.

It's funny how people come into your life, quite un-
expectedly, and end up influencing what comes next.
I certainly hadn't imagined myself writing about a
member of parliament. If anyone had told me that I
was going to make a romantic hero out of someone the
public was holding in such low esteem at the time (I'm
referring to the scandal of MPs' expenses) I'm sure I'd
have backed away as if they were trying to jinx me.
But then I met an MP who was kind enough to offer
a privileged insight into his world and an hour or so
later I realised that a major character – David – was
trying to find his way to me.

Over the past few years I have met more and more
people whose lives have been changed completely
thanks to a condition that almost no family will escape
at some time or another. The way Lisa and David deal
with this cruel turn of fate when it afflicts them, tearing
their dreams apart and leaving them all but helpless
to escape it, forms the main part of the book. This
isn't to say that their story is all struggle and no joy,
because there are plenty of beautiful moments, full of
tenderness and humour, as well as the kind of strength
and togetherness that we would hope for shou[...]

ever find ourselves in their position. It is the relatives of those who have experienced this condition, their courage in the face of tragedy, and loyalty to those they love when they might not even be recognised any more that inspired me to tell Lisa and David's story.

Whenever I write a book it is always with the hope that I will reach someone in a way that will make them feel less isolated or afraid of something life has thrown their way. I want to make them laugh and cry, feel pity and anger, as well as frustration and relief. Above all I aim to give a sense of hope and friendship where sometimes there might seem to be only darkness. Whether or not I succeed only you can say, which is why I would love to hear from you when you've finished reading *Forgotten*. If Lisa and David's experiences touch you as much as I hope they will then please let me know, and perhaps we can share it with others on my Facebook page. Or you can write to me more personally through the Contact link on my website www.susanlewis.com.

Again, thank you for choosing this book and whether you're reading it on the beach or in the bedroom, on a train or a plane, I hope you'll find the journey as engrossing and moving as I did.

Susan

Forgotten

Susan Lewis is the bestselling author of twenty-four novels. She is also the author of *Just One More Day*, a moving memoir of her childhood in Bristol. She lives in Gloucestershire. Her website address is www.susanlewis.com

Praise for Susan Lewis

'A tear-jerker, and a perfect blend of passion, heartache and intrigue' *News of the World*

'Deliciously dramatic and positively oozing with tension, this is another wonderfully absorbing novel from the *Sunday Times* bestseller Susan Lewis . . . Expertly written to brew an atmosphere of foreboding, this story is an irresistible blend of intrigue and passion, and the consequences of secrets and betrayal' *Woman*

'A multi-faceted tear jerker' *heat*

'Spellbinding! . . . you just keep turning the pages, with the atmosphere growing more and more intense as the story leads to its dramatic climax' *Daily Mail*

'One of the best around' *Independent on Sunday*

'Sad, happy, sensual and intriguing' *Woman's Own*

'Mystery and romance *par excellence*' *Sun*

'We use the phrase honest truth too lightly: it should be reserved for books – deeply moving books – like this' Alan

Susan Lewis

Forgotten

arrow books

First published in Great Britain in 2010 by
Arrow Books
Random House, 20 Vauxhall Bridge Road,
London SW1V 2SA

www.rbooks.co.uk

Addresses for companies within The Random House Group Limited
can be found at: www.randomhouse.co.uk/offices.htm

The Random House Group Limited Reg. No. 954009

ISBN 9780099525769

A CIP catalogue record for this book
is available from the British Library

The Random House Group Limited supports The Forest Stewardship
Council (FSC), the leading international forest certification organisation.
All our titles that are printed on Greenpeace approved FSC certified
paper carry the FSC logo. Our paper procurement policy can be found at
www.rbooks.co.uk/environment

 Mixed Sources
Product group from well-managed
forests and other controlled sources
www.fsc.org Cert no. TF-COC-2139
© 1996 Forest Stewardship Council
FSC

Typeset in Palatino by Palimpsest Book Production Limited,
Falkirk, Stirlingshire
Printed and bound in Great Britain by
CPI Cox & Wyman, Reading RG1 8EX